High Desert Guns

High Desert Guns

LAURAN PAINE

Sagebrush
Large Print Westerns

Library of Congress Cataloging-in-Publication Data

Paine, Lauran.
　High desert guns / Lauran Paine
　　p.　　cm.
　ISBN 1-57490-397-7 (lg. print : hardcover)

Due to recent problems with the mail, Library of Congress
Cataloging-in-Publication Data was not available at the time of
publication.

Libraries should call (800) 818-7574 and we will fax or mail
the CIP Data upon request.

Cataloging in Publication Data is available from
the British Library and the National Library of Australia.

Sagebrush Large Print Westerns are published in the United
States and Canada by Thomas T. Beeler, Publisher, PO Box 659,
Hampton Falls, New Hampshire 03844-0659. ISBN 1-57490-397-7

Published in the United Kingdom, Eire, and the Republic of
South Africa by Isis Publishing Ltd, 7 Centermead, Osney
Mead, Oxford OX2 0ES England. ISBN 0-7531-6683-6

Published in Australia and New Zealand by Bolinda Publishing
Pty Ltd, 17 Mohr Street, Tullamarine, Victoria, Australia, 3043
ISBN 1-74030-654-6
Manufactured by Sheridan Books in Chelsea, Michigan.

High Desert Guns

1

"A MAN GETS OLD," HE HAD TOLD THE BOYS THAT DAY back in Missouri when the drought had withered the crops, had bowed down his spirit with misery, had left him viewing all the past hard years of his life with a bleak feeling of futility.

"A man gets old and his soul gets tired."

That was as near as old Ezra Braden ever came to showing defeat although the sour taste of it was in his throat, in his heart, in his big, shaggy old head with its fierce-standing, unkempt hair and beard.

"The time comes when a man's got to move on, boys. When the land turns worthless on him; when he can't n'longer coax life from it. All the days of a man's life that's how it is. Struggle and strain, sweat and hunger."

He was a rawboned, ham-handed old man who had given the long years of his life in the service of the soil. He had once, years back, been a Reb cavalryman and there still lingered some of that erectness, some of that bold-eyed fierceness in him. It had been said in his native Virginia that Ezra Braden had a talent in his hands to winnow out the wickedness from a mean colt or bring life back to the new-born calf. But to look at him now close to his seventieth year, part of the crown missing from his shapeless hat, his cracked old boots nearly sole less, one could easily have mistaken him for another gnarled, toil-worn farmer seeking the end of some private rainbow beyond the wide Missouri. Except for one thing—his eyes.

Ezra sometimes put the thoughtful people he encountered in mind of those oldtime prophets the way

1

he'd stand tall and challenging, green glare hardened against adversity, wild hair stiff standing in a blood-red sunset, thundering denunciation against man and nature, but mostly against man. Then he didn't seem to be an old man so much as he seemed to be a fearful one, and upon the high desert plains of Oregon there were few folks who had ever seen such a fierce old man. He left his impression upon them, as prophets always do, and he also touched their lives swaying them first one way then another way.

He was that kind of an old man; molded in an era of cruel hardship, flame-hardened to his towering strength by the crucible of war, sustained by his powerful will and his uncompromising conviction of what was right in this world, in this life.

He had buried two wives. Each had borne him one son. But now in eastern Oregon where the high desert lay tree-girt and far removed from all the old fealties, he had no wish for another woman; he wished only to prosper, to spend his sundown years in the service of the soil, for after three score years Ezra knew with unshakeable conviction that the less he had to do with mankind the better were his chances to see his sons established and solidly settled before he lay aside his guns and spurs, his vague old memories, and went to his Maker.

Jubal was Ezra's eldest, and Jubal most resembled the old man. He was over six feet tall and rawboned, large-jointed, flinty in his way of speaking and looking at things. At twenty-eight Jubal had been through much of the old man's sufferings; had been there at Misery Bottoms alongside the stinking summertime-sluggish old chocolate-brown Missouri River when his mother had taken the cholera, and had helped the old man bury

2

her. Later, when he was outgrowing clothes like a weed, the old man had taken his second wife. Jubal had been there the night she'd died too, at the birthing of John, old Ezra's youngest.

Life had worked its way with big Jubal; had turned him rock-like in many ways, had blunted any enthusiasm he'd ever possessed, had stilled the forming words in his throat, had put him apart and kept him apart so that even now, in his twenty-eighth year it wasn't easy for him to converse with folks.

But big Jubal had a strong streak of feeling deep down for John, the younger. A man had to feel for *something*. With Jubal it was young John who could bring warmth to his slaty eyes, could bring a faint lilt to Jubal's long, lipless, iron-set mouth.

John was near to six feet like his paw and his brother but he was rounder; there was a good deal of heavy muscle under his smooth hide. He had the strength of two men but John was warm and friendly where the others were not. He laughed often and easily. He wore his six-gun as a man might carry a cross; as something to be borne but never admired. John, at twenty-two, could ride the roughest horse, could lift a yearling high and slam it down at marking time, could carry enough greasewood to the branding fires at one gathering to keep the fires hot all day long.

But John was also the son on whom old Ezra gazed with the most perplexity; he had his dark mother's soft ways; he hated violence, hated fighting, turned away from the blood and the suffering of marking time when they altered the bull calves, cropped off the ears, seared into the living raw flesh with their cherry-red branding irons, and none of this was, in old Ezra's view, the way for a grown man to be.

3

They were at the Blueberry Camp, so called because alongside the hurrying little creek grew wild blue-berries waist-high and dense enough to turn back a charging critter, when Ezra told the boys to change off; said for John to let Jubal rope the next few dozen calves and drag them to the marking grounds for branding and altering and ear-marking.

John had not stepped down but he had heard and let his dark eyes rest steadily upon the old man. This was not the first time down the years Ezra had done this to him. It would not be the last time.

Jubal dashed sweat off his face, looked up, looked around and bent to cut with his bloody knife. "Never mind," he said to the old man. "He's better at the roping anyway."

Ezra squared his shoulders and looked down where Jubal's crimson fingers professionally worked. The calf let off a quavering long bawl. Out with the herd a big freckle-faced Hereford-cross Durham cow slavered and answered, and made a little frantic rush forward. John jumped his horse ahead to block the old cow's rush, first to the left, then to the right, and finally, back into the herd.

"What kind of a man's he going to be?" demanded Ezra of Jubal. "Twenty-one and he's never cut a calf."

"Twenty-two," said Jubal, finishing up. "And cuttin' calves isn't everythin' in life."

"In *this* kind of life it is, Jubal. What kind of cowman'll he end up bein', scairt to whittle on his own bull calves?"

Jubal reached over to cast off the pigging-string, slap the mutilated little animal smartly above the kidneys bringing it to its feet in a bound. He shook off sweat and thoughtfully coiled the little plaited pigging-string. He

4

turned from the waist to signal for John to rope another and drag it over. He said, "Leave him be, paw. 'Isn't a man in the high-country of Oregon who can rope with him or take the snap out of a horse so well. That's somethin'. You can't expect any man to know everything."

"He can learn, Jubal, same as you learned. Same as all of us learn." The old man poked his branding iron fiercely down into the red bed of coals. He was scowling; where skin showed through the hair of his bearded face it was pink from exertion, oily with sweat.

"He can't go along lettin' others do things for him. He's twenty-one now, and a man."

"Twenty-two. Hey, John; fetch us a couple of heifers for a change. I'm gettin' tuckered."

The old man threw up his head to watch John's lariat lift and lightly settle without an inch to spare on either side of its constricting noose. The boy had the grace of his dead mother; he was like her in so many ways. In his warm disposition, in his gentleness, in his sunny laughter and also in the way she shrank from the dark things in life.

How was it possible to sire such opposites as these two stalwart men? Where had his seed failed him in his younger one? Ten generations in the Old Dominion bringing civilization to a bloody land, hammering order out of chaos, had set the iron pattern of his race. But this one—so different; so unexcelled in the things he cared for, so indifferent to the hard, the bitter and painful things he didn't like.

It was, he told himself, and took no solace from it, the workings of God in His all-high wisdom. A man's get was sometimes his pride, sometimes his sore affliction.

"Drag up the next one, boy," he bellowed and averted

5

his head to drop down as John came riding, the stiff-legged fighting heifer-calf at the other, taut end of his lariat.

This was their third year in Oregon. They had prospered here as never before. They had sold none of their cattle or horses. They lived close, saved and scrimped, hunted, trapped, got by well enough too, and now their herd was respectable in size.

They built their squatty, massive log house and log barn that first year. It still served them comfortably although by most standards it was rough and crude enough. When Oregon's redskins came by, always foolish, sometimes fierce, sometimes begging, the old man would run them off. One time he and Jubal faced down a war-party with nothing but two oaken clubs and their stubborn tempers. John had been down after supplies in Salem that time and never did get the straight of that encounter. Ezra shrugged it off as of no consequence. Jubal, because the sons had come to manhood more as friends than half-brothers, said one of the redskins had taken the fringed casing off his rifle to shoot one of the horses tied outside the barn, that the old man had strode over and belted that painted heathen off his horse laying him out stone-cold upon the ground, and when the others would have shot the old man, Jubal said, Ezra strode up to their feathered chieftain, wrenched him off his horse by his braided hair and told him if they ever shot a horse or cow of his he'd come after the lot of them, wipe them out down to the last babe, and to get back on his horse, ride off, and never come near this section of the high desert again.

The Indians had left. To Jubal's knowledge they had never come back.

The old man was like that. He had absolutely no fear

6

and in temper he was a tartar. He could shoot well with either hand and in his prime had once licked four toughs with his fists in a Missouri town. Even in his seventieth year, with prosperity and purpose coming late into his life, he was rawhide-tough and as undeviating as iron.

He worked their branding iron with powerful arms and when the rank smoke of burnt hair and scalded flesh rose up around his face he appeared as some ancient neolithic, or as some mighty Saxon on an alien shore, from times long gone.

He worked there in the hot dust with Jubal, seldom dragging, his sinewy big old arms turned bronze by the high desert summertime heat and fierce glare, an old man who in his sundown years had finally found his place in life, not embittered because it had come so late as most men would have been, because Ezra believed man's lot was hardship and struggle. It had always been that way for him, he expected it to be no different for his sons, so he accepted this late respite without rancor, thinking that all things came to men in God's own good time.

After the last calf had been marked and turned loose he and Jubal stood up to remove their hats and push grimy sleeves across their flushed and sweaty faces. A good day's work had been done here. Jubal swilled water from their jug, totalled up the tally and gave the old man the figures in heifers and bull calves. There was of course some loss: men didn't run cattle in a lawless, wild land without predators getting their share. Every spring the mountain lions, wolves, coyotes, slunk around the calving grounds and three men with rifles—or a hundred and three—couldn't have prevented some loss. Still, the increase over the previous year was impressive, so, while John cared for his horse, Ezra and

7

Jubal went over alongside the creek where their wagon was, to wash up and start the cooking-fire, satisfied, tired, and hungry, but most of all, satisfied. Next year they would have a trail-herd ready. Next year the fruits of their labors would be money and new clothing, a visit to the towns, the good feeling which came from having gold in one's pockets.

2

THE BLUEBERRY CAMP, AS THEY CALLED IT, WAS SET against a tree-tiered mountainside. South, east and west of it, was the endless flow of the high desert. This entire world was an insular place where strangers never appeared, where nothing had changed since the Beginning, and where no man without unswerving purpose would stay for long.

And yet it was, in its own wild way, a pleasant spot. Not just because of the frothy little whitewater creek rushing past, but also because it was cool in the trees, secluded, endlessly hushed, and restful. They ate supper and afterwards sipped black coffee feeling blissfully tired but deeply contented. Because it was a warm night they let their fire die down to cherry-red little coals. The old man filled his stubby buckthorn pipe from a buckskin pouch, dropped a tiny coal into its bowl and puffed away. The smell was both pungent and pleasing at the same time. Indians called that half-tobacco, half-weed, 'Kinnikinnick'. There was a hairy-leafed plant that grew better than six feet tall which was called 'Indian tobacco', but the old man scorned the thing. Some settlers smoked it, usually when they ran out of Kinnikinnick before it was time to go down to the towns in the early spring or in the late fall, but ordinarily white men shunned the weed saying it was fit only for Indians.

The old man was a Virginian with a Virginian's mighty pride. What he thought of Oregon's Indians was a caution; he'd give up his pipe entirely before he'd sink to the level of smoking Indian tobacco.

His pride kept him from taking the ancient hunters' trail on up through the northward mountains too, although he knew as well as his boys also did, that somewhere over through that pass was a new settlement of emigrants.

"Let 'em look to their ways," he growled at John once when the subject of being neighborly had come up, "and we'll look to ours. There's plenty for us to do here. In all my life mixin' with outlanders never brought me to anything but grief. It was strangers comin' on in their wagons brought the cholera which carried off your maw. We'll stay on our side and they can stay on their side; the mountains are high enough. Let them stand between us."

The old man didn't know that John had once gone over there. Jubal knew it because Jube had been waiting in the barn that fourth day when John returned. Jubal had hunted those mountains too; it didn't take a good shot with a good rifle any four days up in there to fetch home a pack-animal laden with fresh meat.

"You been to that emigrant camp," Jubal had growlingly accused his half-brother in the gloomy log barn, and John had turned his dark gaze on big Jubal to say, "That's right, I been to the emigrant settlement, only it's not a camp now; they've built some stores and houses and such-like. They've even got a main road and a saloon."

"The old man'll skin you alive," grumbled Jubal, and

9

he had stalked on out of the barn. John had worried for three days afterwards but Jubal had never told Ezra; Jubal knew his younger brother. Punishment didn't trouble him nearly as much as worrying always did, so Jubal let him sweat those three days, and afterwards, to Jubal's knowledge anyway, John had never again gone 'over the hill' as the old man called it.

Their homeplace wasn't far from where the old Indian trail came down through the mountains from that pass, and in fact that had been one reason why they'd decided to make their headquarters-establishment over there; because the slope was gentle and protective; because that ancient trail meant this was excellent hunting country. Finally, because there was a fine, year-round creek over there too, along with a seemingly endless supply of wood for buildings, for fires in wintertimes, and for the corrals they'd built.

The homeplace was seven miles from Blueberry Camp. In the spring and early summer, which was now, there was a carpet of grass richly covering that entire distance, and much farther, where their herd ranged. A man could look farther, could cross many a spiny mountain range, without finding another place equal to this high desert country for their purpose and for their wants. Regardless of whether they were at the home place or up here in Blueberry Camp, they knew peace and rough contentment, the two things old Ezra had been seventy years seeking.

He sat now, puffing contentedly, letting his harsh memories have their way with him, and it was almost, in this peaceful atmosphere, as though all that bleakness and struggle and anguish had scarred the soul of another man who was now a stranger to him. He recalled with painful vividness two burials and two high moments of

10

a harsh life brought low beside those two graves in widely divergent places. He recalled the years of wandering, of derision from folks in the settled places he'd passed through with his small sons and his worthless old wagon and team. He recalled first noticing the difference in his boys, and it all ran together forming a pattern towards where he now was, leading him to believe that this had all been God's method of putting him through the fires of temptation and agony so that he might emerge a cleansed man in his late years, fit to guide his sons towards a better life in this high desert country. And there was solace in his thoughts, as well as sadness, for old Ezra was a devout man in his own strange way, and took his God to the fields with him every day, on his hunting trails and to his smoky little campfires too, as now.

But Ezra Braden's god was not a benign old white-whiskered gent with a trident and a look of compassion. His god was a lord of war who stalked over mountaintops with a musket and a belted hatchet, a fleshing knife and a bullet mold. His god had the rankness which came from squatting around a hundred campfires in a wilderness full of violence. He was a bearded, fierce old god who hated sin more than he cherished mercy, who despised weakness in man or beast, who viewed without compromise all the temptations which beset the flesh. He was, in short, a god molded after the unrelenting visions the old man himself had always had, and therefore, he was in fact no god at all, but rather he was a dim image of old Ezra himself, which has always been the kind of a god strong, fierce men have always worshipped.

He was a god who could ponder John's aversion to violence and find it unsettling to behold, because as god

11

knew, there had always been violence and there always would be violence, therefore a man grown mature must be prepared to give violence exactly as he must be prepared to face it. What was a little spilt blood or a little agony, if in the end the good work was finished?

He knocked dottle from his pipe, looked across from beneath shaggy brows and said, "Tomorrow we'll head on home. There are the stud colts to be altered when we get back. John, you'll take care of that while Jubal an' I take the teams into the mountains to snake down winter wood."

Jubal, seeing their dying campfire's light redly reflected off the old man's little wet, pale eyes, held his peace and thoughtfully sipped his coffee. John thought, stared straight over at the old man, his belly knotting at the thought of what he'd have to do. But the iron look was upon old Ezra's face; there would be no arguing, and even if there had been, there would be no temporising, no change in that decision. When the old man arrived at his slow judgments nothing in heaven or on earth could move him from them.

John reached for their whisky jug, liberally laced his coffee and drank. His eyes over the tin rim of the cup met Jubal's gray stare; for perhaps half a minute those two looked, said nothing, and understood. The old man hadn't been able to bring John to the marking fire at Blueberry Camp for a very elemental reason: Neither he nor Jubal could work the herd or rope calves nearly as well as John, but it had rankled in the old man's breast that John hadn't stained his hands with the blood or choked on the smoke from burning flesh and hair. Now, he was evening that up. He would have his way after all. He was like that and nothing could change him. Nothing *ever would* change him.

12

They kicked out their rolled blankets upon spongy pine needles, drenched their little fire and bedded down. Up through the stiff tree limbs the sky turned purple, turned almost black. Its promise was like a salve to the troubled minds of men. It caught at a man's mind, at his imagination, carried him along through the long moments before he fell asleep, turning his body all loose and easy, cradling his soul in its ageless promise, encouraging him to think of gentle things until the resentment died away leaving behind only a drowsy awareness of how life should be not how it was.

They were up and stirring ahead of the dawn sunlight. Hitched the team, struck their camp and the old man rode down out of Blueberry Camp with one booted foot braced upon the wagon's dashboard, tooling the lines with the hard wisdom gained through near seventy years of handling teams.

Jubal and John rode along astride their saddle animals whisker-stubbled, compactly sturdy, one fair and one dark.

"A good spring," stated Jubal without glancing over. Without mentioning what he knew was uppermost in his brother's mind. "A good tally. Next year we make up our herd and drive 'em down to the settlements."

"Jube; how old does a man have to be before he says —go to hell?"

Jubal's gray eyes swung, his square jaw took on its solid thrust. "You do it," he said, softening his tone a little so the old man couldn't hear. "You make up your mind he said it's got to be done, and you do it. I know how it is with you—but it's not like you haven't ever cut colts, John, and it's one of those things fellers got to do—so they just do it."

"He knows it near' makes me sick, Jube."

13

Jubal, of the pair of them was most nearly under the old man's sway. He might think bitter thoughts of old Ezra now and then, but he'd never voice them. "There are only three stud colts, John. We'll be gone with the teams for two days or more. Just set your mind to it an' do it."

"I could tell him to go to hell."

"You listen, John: For near' thirty years now the old man's done his best by us. He's done a thousand chores he despised doin' just so's you'n I'd have this chance in life. You think he's any different than you in what he doesn't like to do? He isn't an' neither am I. So where's your right to tell him to go to hell?"

John considered his horse's little bobbing ears; he gazed southward where the high desert ran on towards a dim merging with some vague, heat-hazed mountains in the blue-blurred distance. He hitched at his holstered .45 and his sagging shell-belt. He knew Jubal was correct in all he'd said but still, that didn't change anything; sometimes men are born with a hard aversion and he had his, had always had it. Once, the old man had cut him hard with some harsh words. He'd said: "Your maw was gentle too, boy, and gentleness isn't a good thing for folks like us. It's hardness that counts in this life. What gives you the right—or her either—to think this is a good life with a place in it for tenderness? It isn't— and she died at twenty-seven believing the wrong things matter."

They were passing along the foothills bearing westerly now, with the curving slopes on their right, the plain upon their left. It was still cool and somewhere off in the forested east sunrise was coming strongly with its flaring yellow light to brighten their lower down foothill world.

John rode along full of stillness. It was one of the idiosyncrasies of the high desert country that it could reach deep inside a man bringing him to long, long periods of full silence.

They were a mile off with the foothill-notch visible along the curving foothills where the homeplace was, when Jubal said roughly, "The old man's known how it's been with you since we were buttons, John, and don't think it hasn't been a tribulation to him. Ten dozen times he's given me the sorry end of things to spare you. But there comes a time when that won't go down any more. You're twenty-two now. You've got responsibilities." Jubal paused to turn his head. "How d'you expect to get along in this cattle business if you're scairt of blood and slobberin' critters at markin' time?"

"Who said I had to get along in this cattle business?" John retorted, meeting his brother's level gaze. "Who ever said I wanted to, Jube?"

Jubal rode along for a hundred more feet looking shocked. "Wanted to?" He finally exclaimed. "Had to? Are you sayin', boy, this isn't the life for you?"

"Jube, I don't know." John was torn by indecision, by uncertainty. "I like most of it; it's good to be with stock an'—well—you'n paw. But . . ."

"Yes?"

"Well. I just don't know."

"I see," said Jubal quietly, and looked flintily on up where old Ezra was beginning to cut wide out around a little jutting lip of foothill-land for the big turn up into their ranch roadway.

"No you don't see. Neither does the old man. All you two think of is work and sweat and . . . Listen, Jube; how long did it take you to know what it was you wanted from life?"

15

Jubal didn't answer. In fact he didn't even look around again. He paced on after the wagon, made the identical big turn although with a saddlehorse such a wide maneuver wasn't at all necessary, and he afterwards passed on into the dusty yard.

At the barn the old man stepped down, walked on to the team's head and started loosening harness snaps and straps. Jubal and John swung down and led their saddle animals into the barn for the off-saddling.

John cast a troubled gaze across leather over at Jubal, but the older man's face was locked down against him; Jube went about the unsaddling as though John didn't even exist.

Ezra brought the team in, stalled them and forked hay to them. He said they'd unload the wagon later; right now they'd fix their noonday dinner. He walked off. So did big Jubal.

John watched them cross the yard with their backs to him.

3

THE HOUSE WAS A ROUGH, LONG, LOW STRUCTURE made of peeled logs thick as a man's middle and chinked with 'dobe mud that needed resetting every couple of years. The barn too was of logs and chinking, but it was loftier with big, dowelled-in smooth-adzed rafters and gigantic baulks.

There was a solid air of thrifty accomplishment to the Braden ranch, and yet it wasn't like ranches in other parts of the West, for, although it too had been built with a view to defensive action, with loopholes and water-barrels handy should redskins decide to have a try

16

at murdering its people, it somehow reminded a viewer of an alien establishment in the lawless land; there was something about it which said emphatically the men living here were hard and ruthless in their honest way; were not of the easygoing breed of cowmen who'd long since tamed this trackless world. There was an iron-bottomed plough leaning beside the barn and there was a faggot fence around a garden patch; these were the symbols of grangers, not cowmen. The signs of hoe-men, not cowboys. But the spidery network of peeled-pole corrals spoke of cattle in large numbers, so this was, after all, a working cow ranch.

But the old man had started life with a hoe in his hands. He couldn't stand idly by in the fecund springtime without feeling a powerful urge to stir the soil, to bring forth new life. So each spring he put in his garden patch.

Jubal though, while he infrequently cared for their melons and corn and squash plants, had a lot less feeling for this kind of work than his father. It was John who had a way with growing things, of which old Ezra approved. It was John who had budded their young wild apple trees bringing them to full, sweet fruition. It was also John who diverted part of Braden Creek, as they called the tumbling, brawling waterway behind the house, bringing it over to serve the trees and their vegetable patch. John could coax life from the soil even better than the old man could, which was unusual because the old man knew the earth; knew its temperaments, its vagaries, its moods, better than most men did.

John was setting his irrigation checks the third morning after they'd returned from Blueberry Camp when Jubal and the old man hitched the teams to

17

stripped-down running gear, put axes and crosscuts upon the high wagon seats, and lugged out the heavy logging chains. Ezra, seeing John at his irrigating, said, "Jubal; go tell him we'll be back in a day or three."

That's all the old man said but Jubal knew what had been left unsaid. He walked on down where John was working, leaned across their faggot gate and soberly eyed his half-brother.

"We'll be hauling out now, John. Paw says to tell you we'll be back directly. Two, three days maybe."

John leaned across his shovel. There was a genuine affection between these two but with Jubal it was hard to show soft feeling at any time. He was in this, like the old man.

"I'll do it," John said. They both knew what he meant. "But, Jube, I've been thinking. Maybe I ought to saddle up and ride on from here."

Jubal said nothing. His silence ran on for a long time before it broke. "It'll be the same any place you go, John. It's not *here* or *us* that's troublin' you."

"No?"

"No, boy. It's *you*. Moving on won't change anything. It's you that's got to learn to see life as it is. You're the one, John, not life."

"Maybe, Jube. Still; we'll talk about it when you get back."

"Paw'll likely kick up a rumpus, John. You want to think strong on it, boy."

"I'll have three days, Jube." John picked up his shovel and started along the little irrigation ditch watching his chuckling water rush past. He stopped. Jubal was still leaning there watching him, his long, sun-darkened face, grave. "You be careful up there, Jube. Last summer a falling tree near' got you, remember."

18

"I'll watch. And you—get those colts. They're in the back corral waiting. Be sure of your knots too. A man get a busted skull or broken guts up in here through carelessness and he could die before anyone ever came by."

"I'll make sure."

Jubal straightened back, looked up where old Ezra was fretfully waiting, looked back and said. "We'll be west of the trail if you want us for any reason," then he strode on over to his waiting rig, climbed up, lifted his lines, kicked off the brake and clucked at his horses.

Ezra led out; he knew every switchback and every slope. They'd originally had all the wood they needed right handy to the ranch, but as the years had gone by their cutting circle had steadily moved farther back up into the mountains until, as Ezra had explained, they dared not cut any more trees down close otherwise the winter floods would erode the land and swamp them with mud. A man had to have a feel for the land, Ezra had said. If he lacked that the land would turn against him.

John spent the balance of that day around the garden patch. He watched their little crop stiffen under the hot sun and the cool creek water. He hoed out the persistent weeds and he afterwards, with dusk nigh, carefully secured the gate because every night deer came, drawn by the tantalizing fragrance of those corn rows. Unless a fence was ten feet high the deer would jump it.

He cared for his horse in the barn and afterwards strolled out to where those stud colts were to lean unhappily upon the corral-stringers looking in at them. Like all their horses these colts had been running wild, foraging for their sustenance through tough winters; they were orry-eyed, big and powerful. They had all the

19

instincts of stallions; they would fight a lion or a man with equal ferocity. It was this pride in them he hung back from cutting out. Now, those animals were alive to life in all its many shadings. One month from now their world would be a gray place of everlasting sameness. For pride they would have docility. For temper they would have meekness.

He turned to pass back into the barn on up through and outside into the twilight yard. There was an ancient and moldy old she-bear that hung around close because they frequently fed her. He heard her snuffling whines and grunts coming along through the brambles out back by the creek. She had been trying to snag fish evidently these past few days while they had been over at Blueberry Camp, and now, with the welcome man smell strong in the air again, she was shambling on in to register her complaints at this long neglect.

He went over to the smokehouse where they kept fish and slow elk hanging, cut off several large slices from the ribs and went over by the creek where the old she-gummer was bitterly complaining. The old bear caught her windfall by rearing up on both hind legs like a dancer. She afterwards turned ungratefully and sat down to eat. In her own dim intelligence the days of neglect had turned her sulky, and lacking memory, she couldn't recall any time when these two-legged critters hadn't cared for her.

They'd had a dog once, but he'd very foolishly gone chasing after a scruffy old coyote and had never returned. They'd found him the following spring ripped to ribbons. He'd made a factual discovery too late: A dog fights by lunging at an adversary's throat or ears, and he hangs on with complete stubbornness. A coyote on the other hand doesn't hang on after one bite, he

20

slashes repeatedly, eventually cutting his enemy to bits.

They didn't need the dog anyway. Men wise in the ways of the primitive land could tell from the turning of a leaf, the call of night birds, the sudden stillness roundabout, when peril was nigh. Without half trying he became as wary as an Indian, as attuned to his environment. And that was what turned John abruptly stiff standing in the fading dusk when the old she-bear suddenly stood up, tilted her head, rummaged with her weak eyes and sniffed the eastward night. There was something over in the shadowy foothills; something the old gummer found disconcerting.

John watched her briefly, followed out her pointing nose, saw nothing and heard nothing, but he knew as surely as he knew anything that there was danger over in the easterly forest. Not just from watching the bear, but also because there wasn't a sound over there, and stillness in its own way was as full of warning as a scream. Birds, garrulous by nature and gregarious by instinct, inhabited the foothill forests; they were never silent, but now they were. So were the other little creatures which lived up in those ranks of gloomy pines and firs.

He stepped inside, took down a .30-.30, levered a shell into its chamber and stepped back out onto the porch again. Occasionally an old lion, too slow and awkward for a fast kill, ventured down out of the high country seeking newborn calves or colts. Those old cougars were the dangerous ones. Young lions avoided men and grew sleek off deer and elk. The old ones, unable to outrun fat does, forced to live on rabbits and lesser critters, became desperate in time; they would attack a man.

He stepped off to the side of the house when their old

she-bear suddenly dropped down on all fours and went scuttling back around to the creekside brambles, making her snuffling, bleating sounds of fear and anxiety. It was enough to make the hair at the base of a man's skull stand straight up. If it had been broad daylight the fear wouldn't have been so unnerving, but in the half-light of evening visibility was limited.

He waited, scarcely breathing; made himself blend in with the descending night. He watched that eastward flow of land going over in his mind the places over there where an enemy might be hiding, might be this very moment, watching him from cruel eyes.

It was a long wait. The night came closing in, the silence continued to pulse. That total silence, over there also remained, which meant that whatever was over there hiding, had made no move to depart.

One of the stud colts out back threw up its head and softly nickered, which was not the sound a frightened horse would make at all, and this briefly puzzled John. If that was an old lion crouched over there the horses would be in a frenzy. If they made any noise at all it would be their shrill, trumpeting whistle of fear and peril. He stepped back a little farther to get deeper into the pool of blackness made, by the side of their house. He didn't think that was a lion over there after all. He thought it was a man; that the whinnying colt had smelled another horse. It followed logically enough that if there was a horse over there which could not walk on out into the clearing as any loose horse would have done, it was simply because there was also a man over there, and he wouldn't permit his horse to be seen.

He wished Jubal and old Ezra were close by. He also tried to recall some of the tales they'd all heard of outlaws in the high desert country. But in three years

22

they'd spoken to only a few travelers, mostly restless hunters or trappers in wintertime, and they'd never actually seen any skulking men near the ranch at all.

Then the gunshot came. He felt as though something white-hot had cut into his soft parts. His breath burst out in a swift explosion of soundlessness. A pain increased steadily in his back. He began to feel faintness. He dropped the .30-.30 and fell into the rearward rough log wall. His right leg was stiffening. Waves of cold and burning heat raced through him, blue motes danced in front of his eyes. He struggled against easing downward but it happened in spite of his desperate efforts. He slid straight down the log wall and fetched up in a sitting position. He no longer had any power in his limbs and although the breath came back it pained him terribly to breathe. He closed his eyes and ground his teeth. He moaned slightly and thought: *God I'm shot; I'm dying!*

As he sat there sunk and crumpled, came the soft sound of voices out of the eastward distance; the gritty rustle of booted feet grinding across the dusty yard towards him in the darkness. He shrank within himself. He opened his dulling eyes with a powerful effort for there was a strong lassitude in him now, a spreading, pleasant warmth that turned him weak as a kitten.

There were three of them, all tall, lanky men dressed as cattlemen in rough shirts and faded pants with brass cartridges in their belt loops and with .30-.30s in their hands. They had six-guns too, but they stood above him gazing down with only their Winchesters in hand. They were rough, fierce-looking men with sun-blackened, weathered faces and a solid stamp of evil imbedded in their features. They were gaunt and unkempt as though long on some secret trail. One of them—a man with a little crescent scar above his right upper lip—said,

23

"Plumb through an' through. Pretty good shot if I do say so myself, it bein' dark an' all."

One of the others bent, caught up John's gun, examined it briefly and hurled it away. The third one peered closer. This one said in a piping voice, "He ain't dead yet."

The crescent scarred man shrugged. "He will be. They don't hang on long with a hole like that in 'em. You two go on in and hunt for the cache. Three years of livin' here 'thout sellin' cattle or even once hittin' the towns except for flour'n coffee means they got a poke of gold hid here somewhere. Go find it if you got to tear the damned house down. Go on."

The pair of men moved off leaving that scarred man standing still, gazing upon young John. This man leaned aside his carbine, went to work making a smoke, and when he afterwards lit up to touch the cigarette's tip he also bent downward and put the little pinprick of yellow light to John's face. There was no quick contraction from the dilated night-darkened pupils. The man straightened back, put out his match and dropped it. He took a big sweep of smoke deep into his lungs, turned and thoughtfully gazed around. Perhaps that poke was hidden in the barn somewhere; he'd go look over there while his pardners ransacked the house.

He smoked on for a moment, dropped a final last casual look downward and beheld the still, gray face down there. John was dead. The stranger picked up his .30-.30 and went sauntering across to the barn.

4

OLD EZRA STOOD THERE IN THE HOT DUST OF LATE afternoon his face terrible in its grief and its wildness. He didn't make a sound. Over in front of the barn Jubal turned to say thinly, as though some premonition had affected his normally deep-timbered voice. "He hasn't fed the horses out back either; looks like he's been gone maybe two days, Paw."

The old man stood on, feeling the sands of life running out, stood there gazing at that swollen 'thing' seated with its thick shoulders slumped against the log side wall of their house. The old man had no mind for the tiredness weighing down his seventy-year-old frame. He was numb to the bruises of their labor at getting the logs sawed and chained to the wagon beds. Time was standing still for him. He could have been gone from here for a year or a minute; everything was telescoped into this one awful moment while he stood there gazing down at dead John with that ragged, gaping bullet hole in his middle.

Why? Who had done such a thing? What reason, what purpose? Dark John with his maw's gentle ways; he'd driven off from the lad with his aloofness between them, unwilling to turn and wave back, and this too lay leaden in his heart: that he'd parted from his last-born with a coolness between them.

It didn't matter that the boy didn't want to see blood or cruelty; it didn't matter that he shrank from violence and harshness. If God would just give him back . . . just give him back this doe-eyed one who was so like his mother had also been, so gentle and smiling.

25

"*John!*"

The old man finally lifted his terrible face. Jubal was there standing like stone holding that .30-.30 he'd found lying off a ways.

"Paw—for God's sake—*he's been shot!*"

Ezra turned and placed his back to his dead son. There was a terrible hurt squeezing the life from his heart. An almost unendurable pain of loss, of tearing agony. The afternoon was fast fading but he scarcely noticed. Over in front of the log barn the teams stood patiently awaiting the unharnessing, their loads of limbless logs chained high and hard. Over the rim of the northward mountains there was no sun now, only the sky, red as blood. Swiftly he walked around to the front door, which hung open, and cast his milky gaze at the wreckage and the havoc visible inside. He stepped in, turned from the waist left and right, spied a dusty big bootprint and looked long at it before turning and retracing his steps back out into the crimson yard. He quartered like an old hunting hound on a scent; passed this way and that until he came to a straight trail leading eastward. There, he found the place thirty feet inside the trees where three horses had stood, where three men had crouched.

This was his work. He was wise in the ways of tracking; had been clever at it since earliest boyhood in the sweetgrass Virginia countryside. He walked on parting underbrush here, ducking around low limbs there. And he made good time because the ground was spongy in here, took tracks well and held them.

He found where, a mile northward, those three men had left the northward trace to cut over into the forest. They had deliberately done this; they had known right from the start what they were up to. Thieves and

26

murderers, those three, and unless they took wing he'd track them down.

But when the last light failed, forest gloom deepened all around, he marked the spot with a blaze where he'd take up this trail again, and started heavily back. It was near nine o'clock. He'd been gone five, six hours, he neither knew how long nor cared; there was an emptiness in him as hollow as a deadfall log.

Jubal had attended the burying. He was standing at the mound dark with the sweat of his labors, bare-headed, big and mighty and shaggy, a replica of the old man only many years younger. He had hold of himself by then and turned as Ezra strode up.

"Say the word over him, Paw, an' what did you find on the trail?"

"The trail will keep," murmured the old man gazing with hard eyes upon that fresh-turned moldy earth. "John my son grace to you and peace from God the Father and our Lord Jesus Christ who gave Himself for our sins that He might deliver us from this evil world, according to our God and Father to whom the glory be for ever an' ever. The Lord will ravish the soul of those that spoiled thee, son, and I will be His instrument. Peace be with you in His gilded towers. Amen."

He walked off to be by himself, an old man full of years, unkempt, calloused but unbent by labor; sat out there behind his log barn with the sounds of Jubal freeing the patient beasts from their harness and their heavy loads round front, dropped his bearded face into both hands and wept, and afterwards with his mouth tightened by bitterest melancholy, he prayed for a sign, for guidance from his particular god, who was a vengeful and a terrible, a striker-down of the iniquitous, a trampler upon of the evil afflicted, a lord of war who

27

strode across mountains armed and full of wrath against the evil doer.

It was close to midnight before he went back to the burial site and stood shock-headed and loose-shouldered to offer his final prayer before passing on to the house where Jubal was sitting in total darkness amid the wreckage, and lit a lamp to make coffee by. By then his first frightful shock had passed; he was himself again, only more so. There was a swollen sense of destiny riding his spirit now. It was his sign from on high. As he'd said at the graveside *he* would be His instrument in exacting harsh justice.

He took a cup of coffee to Jubal who refused it, and in a low, intense way he insisted, pushing forth the cup. "Take it and drink it, boy. The trail will be a long one I think, and without strength we'll never complete it. Drink the coffee and sleep, if you can. We ride at first light."

Jubal took the cup and drank. He afterwards watched the old man oiling his Winchester and running the same rag over his rebored old .44 long-barrelled Dragoon pistol. "Where did the trail lead, Paw?" he asked, finally. "How many were there?"

"There were three of them, Jubal, an' their trail come on over the hunters' trail from the north. They went into the forest a mile or such a matter northward. They knew what they were about."

"Perhaps from the settlement, Paw."

"It's possible. I've told you—both—many times; nothing but evil comes out of men all herding up together in towns and the like. What wars have ever been started by men in the country? None! What murder and thievin' and purest evil was ever originated out in the land? None!"

28

"They were hunting for something, Paw."

"I know. Gold. They thought we had gold cached." The old man stopped busily wiping weapons long enough to raise his head and show Jubal by weak lamplight the dark, stirring, mysterious things moving in the depths of his wild stare. "It's an old, old story, Jubal; men prospering being jealously spied upon by the reavers of this world who would wantonly kill to take what others had gotten by their sweat and pain."

"We have no gold, Paw."

"No. They didn't have to kill to find that out. They could've struck him down, or they could have plundered the place first while keeping him under their guns. No man of principle kills like that. I know; I've seen it hundreds of times in war. You hold another man's life in your gun hand; it's perfectly right to pull the trigger. But you don't; you hold him helpless but you don't wantonly kill. Even a coyote doesn't do that; not the meanest of animals kills out of hand. Now you'd best get some sleep. We'll be heading over the mountains ahead of the sun."

Jubal got stiffly up and crossed over to place his cup upon the sink and turn there leaning with his narrow hips against the rough wood watching his father. Filling the orange-lighted low room was a throbbing solitude. Outside an old yellow moon floated silently overhead faintly brightening an otherwise darkened world. Wolves traveling in their lolling-tongued fashion paused atop some spiny ridge to yank up stiff-legged and make their eerie cry which was full of a loneliness as old as time. Then they ran on again in that endless quest which motivated all wolves.

Jubal paced across to the door and stood a long time in the opening gazing northward, up where a brooding

29

peak near the top-out of the hunters' trail became a moonlighted, brooding witch's hood, dark-shadowed and bowed with a grimness. He felt a midge in a vastness, an insignificant mote in the star-washed timeless and endlessness of infinity. Tomorrow they'd go, carrying guns. They would track those three with one depthless virtue they shared, Jubal and the old man; patience. Endless patience; the kind which created empires and lifted up dynasties, the patience of taciturn rough men turned hard and endlessly persevering by a common wish and a common grief.

Whatever the old man felt about being His instrument, Jubal, standing there in the cool night gazing out, felt no such burning zeal at all; he felt only the wish to kill three men for a senseless murder which had deprived him of one of the very few things in his life he'd ever been able to pour out his dammed-up affection upon. Everything else, their holdings, their herd, their unswerving purpose up to now, fell away from Jubal as a bad dream. He remembered only his brother's grimace-frozen face and the black stain spilt downward from his vitals soaking the soil. The old man had time and again cautioned them against softness; against expecting anything from this lifetime but hardship and struggle. He had once, within Jubal's hearing, upbraided gentle John for thinking there should be gentleness in this world. He'd said, that time, that John's mother had died believing in things that didn't matter. Well; now John had died believing in the same things.

Ezra put aside his guns and rose up to consider his eldest in the open doorway. "Sleep, boy," he rumbled. "The chance may be a long time coming for us again."

"When I'm ready I'll bed down," Jubal answered, and

30

old Ezra, in the act of turning towards his plundered bunk, swung back. Jubal, most under his sway, had rarely spoken up to him in this manner. He hung there pondering: This was not a normal time for either of them. Jubal was a man grown and matured. He had his ways too, exactly as the old man had his, so in the end Ezra said nothing, but went on over to his bunk and lay back fully attired staring up at the sooty log rafters.

He could recall as vividly as though it had been only yesterday John's mother with her smile and her good, soft roundness. In his private heart he could remember each time they had come to one another, man and wife, and how her doe-brown liquid soft eyes had nearly drowned him in love and tenderness.

But those times, like all the other high moments in the old man's life had been all too brief, all too quickly swamped under the grinding adversity which He sent to test and temper Ezra. But a man with a powerful yearning, even though he resisted it with all his might, was sorely tempted to cry out against that endless tribulation, for what did it get a man of flesh and blood, that although he be fit to enter the Kingdom of God, all the days of his earthly existence be spent in anguish and deprivation and tragedy?

Sleep wouldn't come. Not for Ezra, not for mighty Jubal. The night passed silently along beneath its sprinkling of stars and its yellow old lopsided moon. Along towards morning the old man dropped off, but Jubal never did. His was the younger and therefore tougher frame; it could be swayed from natural need by imagination and all the bitter, terrible loneliness which stretched ahead for Jubal without young John.

A man comes to full maturity accepting almost without question certain established things, and so it

31

was with Jubal. He couldn't think of sleep because gradually as the night wore on towards pre-dawn, the realization firmed up through the stunned, near disbelief, that one of the things—the *foremost* thing— he'd accepted unquestionably as always being close by, was suddenly gone. Totally, entirely gone.

It took a lot of getting used to, particularly for a man such as Jubal Braden in whom there was a certain heaviness, a certain fatalism, which accepted things as they were—not as they became suddenly and irrevocably, altered. He would not entirely return to normal for a long time. It was as though a part of him had been swiftly cut away leaving behind the numbness and the dullness of an endless ache which could not immediately heal nor depart.

He got up when the first pale, steely light appeared, made fresh coffee, rolled an oily bag of jerky into a blanket, drank the coffee, took up his guns and went on outside.

This was the coolest part of any summertime day, this hour or two ahead of sunrise when dew made pearls in the spiderwebs and clean, washed air came steadily down through that slot in the mountains where the hunters' trail cut between brooding peaks. It was also the best time for a man's rest, so Jubal let the old man sleep on while he rigged out their saddle animals, went over to open the corral gate for those stud colts to run back to the high desert because there was no way to tell when they might ever return to this place—if they ever did.

He also turned loose the teams and heaved out behind the barn a bag of rock salt. He did this without thinking. It was instinctive to throw salt out so that the animals would come back often to lick it. That was how a man

32

kept track of his critters. It was also how he found them without much trouble after he'd been away a long time.

Ezra came to life finally, ran bent fingers strokingly through hair and beard as was his custom, washed at the kitchen basin and walked outside with his dully-shining, freshly cleaned and oiled weapons. He said nothing as he went up to his saddled, waiting beast, slung the .30-.30 from its place under his right leg, felt the cinches out of lifelong habit and caution, stepped up over leather and without a look or a word struck out on up the hunters' path northward.

Jubal was a moment or two behind the old man. He had to make fast that greasy cloth bundle of jerky aft of the cantle. But he caught up where the old man waited at the tree-blaze. From here on they were riding a strange, new trail.

5

THEY BREASTED THE TOP-OUT WITH THE FIRST SOFT light of dawn tinting the highest places palest pink, and they waited a while up there with good warmth loosening their muscles and bringing on a pleasantness which had been lacking to them since the day before. Rearward lay the gloomy forests, the downhill world which passed their cabin dooryard. Ahead, dimly seen hull down out upon a vast prairie, lay a clutch of buildings which looked raw even from this distance, from their peeled newness.

This, Jubal thought, was what fascinated young John; this settlement with its strangers and its gaudy sights. He'd been only a boy when they'd last been in a village. Even when they'd needed supplies from the settlements southward from the high desert, old Ezra had invariably sent Jubal, never young John. It had been almost as though the old man had somehow known evil would reach out for his youngest in one of these places, and Jubal, in his private thoughts, considered it true that this is what had happened that one time John had sneaked away, ostensibly on a hunting trip, to visit that village down there.

He had talked to strangers of their ranch over the mountains, of their cattle perhaps, and the strangers had listened with avarice and speculation. And now John was dead.

"It is a poor place for a settlement," old Ezra observed from their eminence as he gazed down at that soft-lighted, distant place. "They'd have done better to build up closer to the foothills where there's wood and creek water."

That was all the old man had to say about the place as he set his horse to the long descent downward, with new light beginning to yellow the peaks and filter down onto that vast prairie where shadows still heavily lay.

It took an hour of steady riding just to leave the hills behind and feel a levelling off of their tilted-up descending mounts, and by then dawn was fully over the world with its cleanliness and its promise of later on heat.

They nooned at an old Indian camp where black stone-rings lay at random proving that this had been a favorite site with the vanished red men in eons gone. There was a good spring here and the old man shot two blue grouse which they roasted in total silence at one of the stone-rings.

It was hot out on this prairie; much hotter even than their own high desert country across the mountains.

34

They felt this heat. It wilted them a little and made the old man drowsy when they rode on again. He dropped off from time to time as they resumed their way, jerking awake when his slackening body sagged off-balance.

Jubal sweated but felt no need for sleep nor rest. He kept studying their onward destination. There would of course be a lawman at that place. He knew from what John had said there was a saloon down there too. For the rest though, he had only his own eyes as guides, but they were good enough.

The town lay flat out upon the plain. There was a clump of alders and cottonwoods at the upper, or northern end of it where Jubal thought must be a spring, for otherwise there was no indication of water and regardless of what other motivation settlers ever had for putting their settlements where they did, they always had to consider water foremost.

The roadway was broad and functionally ugly in a sere, raw wood way. Stores were mostly of peeled log, but occasionally he caught sunlight's dull flash off tin roofs and even off dirty white tent-top canvas.

Around the town in every direction excepting eastward—the direction they were riding from—were square log houses with here and there a barn and an occasional fenced-in plot where a milk cow grazed or some sheep ran in their foolish, bleating way. Nearly every residence had its garden patch, even the homes close to town had patches of sturdy vegetables.

The first sounds they heard when they came over onto the north-south wagon road was of barking dogs and of hammers striking wood. This place obviously was still growing. There was a circled-up wagon camp a mile off over near the eastward curve of mountains. Newcomers evidently who had not yet chained out their homestead

35

plots nor entirely lost the habits which made wagoners reluctant to abandon their homes on wheels.

Somewhere too, a blacksmith was at work upon his anvil. This was a good sound, a musical sound that rose up into the still, summertime air like cathedral music, peal after peal of it.

Closer still, they could see people moving here and there, passing in and out of those raw-fronted stores, often hurrying, frequently hurrying along only to halt when they encountered others, to stand in overhang-shade, talking.

The place had a bustle to it, a snap and whiplash quality which left Jubal wondering why all the haste? Three high-sided freight outfits were camped just north of town upon the tall-grass prairie. These would be the village's lifeline; the means for bringing in the goods without which no town, frontier or otherwise, could survive.

Two boys furiously at work digging out a badger in his den paused to watch the old man and Jubal ride by, their faces alive to any kind of newness, their blue eyes brightly probing.

The old man stopped. "What is the name of your town?" he quietly asked.

One of the boys, a freckle-faced youth in his early teens, answered up in a cracking voice. "Jefferson, sir. It's named after Thomas Jefferson."

"Thank you," said the old man in that same inflexionless, quiet tone. "And do you have a constable in Jefferson?"

"Yes sir, we got one. His name's . . ." The boy's eyes slowly widened as an obvious thought struck him. "Mister; you in trouble?"

"His name, boy, his name!"

36

"Bond, sir. Constable Walter Bond. He'll be at the jailhouse supervisin' things. They ain't quite got it finished yet an' he wants 'em to get it done."

"Thank you," said the old man, gravely, and rode on.

Jubal turned once to see those two lads standing back there statue-like, full of youthful curiosity. He straightened forward and went along beside the old man bringing all his attention back upon the town. Now, he could see saddled horses tied along the tie racks. Where the most horses stood he made out a freshly painted rough sign: *Redmond's Saloon.*

That would be the place John had spoken of because, although Jubal looked diligently as they swung on into Jefferson from the southward road, he found no other saloons in the place.

The jailhouse though, was easy to locate; that's where all that hammering they'd heard back a mile was coming from. The front of the building was completed, as near as big Jubal could determine, but around the back where some green rafters stood naked of sheathing for the roof, there was a gaping emptiness. That was where the cells would be, when the building was eventually completed.

They passed dustily along through roadway traffic, two large quiet men, and hitched up outside the new jailhouse. A stocky, sandy-haired man came strolling on over to the rack and nodded at them. "Are you gents lookin' for the law?" he inquired, running an assessing pair of blue eyes over them.

Ezra considered the stocky man's star and his tied-down businesslike gun. "We are," he stated. "I'm Ezra Braden. This is my eldest son Jubal." The old man didn't offer his hand. "Three men shot and killed my youngest son over the mountains a day or two ago.

37

When Jubal and I came back from gathering winter wood we found John beside the cabin shot through."

Constable Bond studied the old man. "I see," he murmured. "You'd be the fellers who have that ranch on the high desert over the hills at the base of the Injun trail. I've heard of you."

Bond and old Ezra stared at one another. Obviously, whatever it was Walter Bond had heard of these two, left him curious and interested.

"Three men you say?"

"We found their sign, sir. There were three of them. They came from this direction."

"Know anything else about them, Mr. Braden?"

The old man shook his head. "They smoked cigarettes. They came over to rob us. They ransacked our house and barn."

"Was your boy shot in the back?"

"He was shot through the middle, Constable. He died hard—and alone."

Bond leaned there upon the tie rack scowling. "There are a lot of strangers around, Mister Braden; some of 'em aren't what I'd call desirable citizens. Some are drifters passin' through. I'll need more to go on than you've given me."

Jubal, standing back in full silence, gazed up towards *Redmond's Saloon.* He had a strong desire to go up there, to ask around if anyone recalled his brother and the men he might have visited with at the bar. But for the time being he did nothing of the kind. Let the old man handle this his way; he was no fool and he knew men.

"Constable," said old Ezra, his voice hardening slightly towards the stocky man, "I expect no miracles. I ask that you name me the names of your troublemakers

38

and I'll find which of them rode over the pass a couple of days back."

Walter Bond put a skeptical look upon the old man. He clearly didn't like the sound of that. "Mister Braden in this place *I* do the questioning for the law. That's an ironclad rule of mine. You two fellers get to pokin' around and you might find more grief than you can handle."

Jubal saw how close these two quite unalike men were to becoming enemies, and said quietly, "Constable, tell me this: Are there three men who run together a lot, maybe like pardners, who could do a thing like this?"

Bond swivelled his blue gaze. He ran a slow look up and down big Jubal. He was a man in his middle or late forties who could have had a son Jubal's age, but in fact he didn't have; he was a widower with only a daughter. "There might be," he replied. "But there are a lot of men who pardner-up out here, Mister Braden, and if you and your paw go around jumpin' the wrong ones you could get killed. I'd suggest a little forbearance to both of you." Bond straightened back off the rack. "Put up your animals, have dinner, cool off a little then come on back. We'll talk about this thing."

"Talk?" said old Ezra, his pale stare turning cold. "There's not much need for talk, Mister Bond. We want three murderers. We aim to get them."

Bond slowly inclined his head. "Include me in that 'we', Mister Braden. Now go do as I say then come back. I won't be idle while you're gone."

Bond turned on his heel and paced over to his jailhouse, stepped inside and passed from sight. Ezra kept looking after him; he seemed of two minds about this meeting.

Jubal unlooped his reins and turned to head northward towards the liverybarn. "Come along, paw, he knows his town and he looks like a man who'll waste little enough time. While we're here we'd best consider what he says."

Ezra turned, also leading his animal, and walked along, but now his head was down, his old eyes were thoughtful behind the droop of heavy lids, and they were sharp as the eyes of a ferret. He knew towns like this one; had been in dozens of them in his time. Sometimes it was prudent to look and listen and say nothing. But it was hard to do; mortal hard. A boy's cooling body under the sod cried out to be avenged.

The liveryman was a harassed, doughty individual by the name of Wilford Cullen. He was a Kentuckian and the moment he opened his mouth old Ezra's gaze settled on him. That Southern drawl and the slurred-over manner in which he sounded some letters in his speech, focused the old man's attention upon him. But right then old Ezra had no time to talk much, Cullen's barn, the only livery stable in town, was noisily alive and bustling. Out the back there was a smithy; that's where the struck-anvil sounds had been coming from Jubal had speculated about on the way into Jefferson.

They handed over their horses and stood a while over by Wilford Cullen's cubbyhole office watching all this activity. To deliberate, unhurried moving men the hustle seemed almost indecent. Men came and went, some seeking the shoeing-shed, some to leave travel-stained horses, others to rent animals, all of them in a hurry. Speech here was brusque, men had no time for the civilities, Cullen himself, a lanky, lean Kentuckian with a big fat nose and little sunk-set observant eyes, appeared to always be on top of whatever happened. In all the time Jubal and the old man stood over there watching, they never once saw the Kentuckian at a loss when someone shouted questions at him or asked for suggestions. And yet Cullen, a gangling man in his sixties, never looked bothered by any of this. Jubal made a mental note to talk to this shrewd looking lanky man. His barn was obviously a hub of activity in Jefferson. If any scraps of conversation were carelessly dropped, it would probably be in Cullen's barn and he would have heard them. He was that kind of a man.

They passed outward as far as the roadway and there halted again. For the first time since leaving the ranch their resolve was diluted a little; it was the noise and activity. As the morning wore along Jefferson became a beehive of constant movement and bedlam. Battered old wagons passed along the roadway, stores were crowded, people called back and forth to one another and summertime dust hung like a blight in the heavy air.

The old man said, "We'll be needing a room. I'll go across to the boardinghouse and see to that. You walk around this place and keep your ears open. We'll meet at Bond's office later."

Jubal was agreeable to this; he thought he understood how it was with old Ezra too. Towns like Jefferson reminded him of other towns in other places; they reached deep down into him bringing back memories. The old man had his many reasons for wishing to be alone for a little while; the impact of noisy civilization required that men much alone grope for their own individual ways of coping with it.

Jubal sauntered northward. Across the road up there was *Redmond's Saloon.*

He was a head taller and near a foot broader than most of the pedestrian traffic pushing southward around

41

him. Although his rugged features were set in their habitual expression of tranquil confidence, he was interested in all this. So interested in fact that a high-breasted tall girl with ash-blonde hair stepping forth from a little store caught him looking the wrong way and plowed ahead behind her loaded arms to bump him squarely and solidly. Although she was tall her weight and impetus only settled big Jubal back on his heels caught low by sharp edges, but the girl almost fell and she dropped her packages.

He caught her arm to steady her, found himself gazing into a startlingly lovely face, and as he released the tall girl's arm he said gravely, "My apologies ma'am. Here; I'll help you with the bundles."

She stood gazing over at him, her eyes darkly angry, her heavy mouth pulled flat, but she didn't speak which was perhaps just as well. She instead bent over and also began gathering the dropped packages, and afterwards, when she had them all again, some of her temper was past and gone.

She said, "Thank you. I suppose it was as much my fault as yours. I could hardly see over the bundles."

Jubal nodded, turned as she moved gracefully around him, set her southward course in the direction of the jailhouse and moved off. She was beautiful, but perhaps, Jubal told himself, any woman with girlhood's freshness still upon her would affect a lonely man the same way. He lost her, finally, among the other pedestrians and turned back to considering *Redmond's Saloon* over across the way.

There was noise coming past the swinging doors and men in the attire of cattlemen and settlers constantly came and went. He could imagine young John entering that place, the first saloon he'd ever been in.

6

REDMOND'S SALOON WAS PERHAPS THIRTY FEET BY thirty feet. It had green sawdust underfoot and a long brass rail the full length of its bar. It hadn't yet acquired that peculiarly masculine smell saloons in cow-towns had, but was well on the way to acquiring it.

The patrons were many and varied. There were thick-shouldered freighters as bearded as old Ezra. There were narrow-hipped rangeriders with their belt-guns and their spurred boots, and also there were townsmen, for thus far anyway, Amos Redmond's barroom was the only saloon in town.

It was a noisy place and the walls trembled from stamping feet and constant movement. What caught and held Jubal's attention as he worked his way over towards the brass rail were two fresh holes in the barfront. He'd seen enough bullet holes to recognize them when he saw them. Evidently Amos Redmond's saloon occasionally had violence amid this noise too.

He bought a glass of tepid beer and stood gazing over the customers. Three men were playing poker at a distant table. One of those men had an unusual little crescent scar at the outer edge of his right upper lip. The others with him were nondescript enough; cowboys from the looks of them, tough and capable. Elsewhere men were playing blackjack at another table; these though were freighters in checkered woollen shirts and low-heeled cowhide boots. They were massive men, these freighters, with lungs of leather and vocabularies to shame the devil himself.

Along the bar were more settlers and cattlemen. Behind it were two men, one slight and wiry and

43

grinning, the other thick-thewed, blocky, and as shapeless as a beer barrel. Jubal heard men call this squatty, immensely powerful man Amos, sometimes they even called him Mister Redmond, but usually it was just Amos.

He kept drifting his gaze back to that burly, stonefaced man. Redmond was one of those rare individuals who, although nature had never endowed him physically for speed or grace, had somehow managed to develop both these attributes. He was light on his feet, moved smoothly, and there was scar tissue over both his deep-set eyes to prove that he'd had reason to move swiftly a few times in his life. Amos Redmond clearly was a fighting man, although Jubal judged him now to be in his early forties. Once, he came over and pointedly gazed at Jubal's empty beer glass. Obviously Amos Redmond didn't encourage loafers to take up bar space unless they were drinking men, or at least *buying* men. Jubal nodded, got a refill, and let it sit there in front of him. He'd never been much a beer man and it was too early for serious whisky-drinking, so he let that glass of beer purchase him additional time at Redmond's bar. He had an idea the crowd might thin out for the midday meal and meant to await that opportunity to talk to Redmond. But, although most of the customers did in fact depart after a while, others came stamping in to take their place.

In the end Jubal had to give it up. He sauntered back out into the roadway sunshine, turned sharply left—and bumped head on into that same lovely girl for the second time. They both took one backward step and gazed steadily at one another.

"It appears," said the girl, studying Jubal's big shoulders, "that we didn't quite make the plankwalks wide enough when we laid out this town."

44

He came near to smiling. She was piqued but only mildly so; Jubal Braden, six feet and two inches tall and better than two hundred pounds in heft, was no mere thing to bump into. He was rock-hard and solid. There was no 'give' in him anywhere, no softness of bone or gristle.

"Well, missy," he quietly stated. "I don't think it's so much a matter of broad enough walkways as it is a matter of lookin' where a body's walking along. My name's Jubal Braden. I'm new to your town."

"I'd never have guessed it," answered the handsome, tall girl, in a droll tone of voice. "I'm Mary Bond, Mister Braden, and perhaps you're right; perhaps I wasn't watching as well as I might've been. I'm sorry— for *both* times."

"Bond?" Jubal murmured. "By any chance related to the constable?"

"His daughter, Mister Braden." She smiled and swept on around Jubal heading northward this time. He turned slowly and watched her move through the sidewalk traffic. He didn't think she resembled her father in the least.

Someone on ahead called up to Jubal fetching his attention back around. It was Ezra, standing down in front of the boardinghouse. The old man looked fresh-scrubbed but otherwise he seemed the same. Jubal went on down and the pair of them struck on over towards the jailhouse where that insistent hammering out the back seemed to be stilled, finally, during the noon hour.

Constable Bond was in his office. He pushed chairs over for the Bradens and seated himself at a makeshift rickety big table piled with weighted-down stacks of papers and wanted flyers. He jumped right into the topic

45

at hand without any preliminaries, giving Jubal the impression that Walter Bond was a man who knew his work and didn't shirk it.

"In a place as new as Jefferson, gents, the surest way to gather information is by talkin' to the established people in business. I've been doing that."

The old man said quietly, "So have I, Constable Bond."

Jubal was surprised at his father; he'd had some notion old Ezra hadn't left the boardinghouse all morning. Bond though, didn't appear surprised at all. He looked upon the old man as though he'd already made up his mind about him.

"I reckon you have, Mister Braden, and I don't expect you found out much."

Ezra sat silent, which meant in fact he *hadn't* found out anything. He and Walter Bond seemed to have entirely forgotten the third man there with them; they eyed each other the same way strange dogs eye one another, half-willing to be civil, half-willing not to be.

"Will Cullen at the liverybarn recalled no particular three men riding in together for the past few days," stated Bond. "Amos Redmond over at the saloon didn't recollect any of our less desirable citizens being gone for as long as it'd take to ride over the mountains, kill your boy, and ride back again." Bond reared back in his chair. "Of course, gents, that's no positive proof at all, but it sort of makes me think maybe those three men didn't come to Jefferson; maybe they were men passing through. We get a lot of that kind."

"I'm sure you do," said the old man quietly. "But I can tell you one thing, Constable—wherever those men *came* from, they rode directly back to your town. I read

46

their sign every mile of the way. They came to Jefferson yesterday sometime."

Bond crossed his legs, clasped both hands over one knee and steadily gazed at the old man. "Anything else?" He inquired. "Mister Braden, I get the feeling you know more'n you've said. Let me tell you again— no private feuds in my town. You want the killers of your boy: Fine. So do I. But if you know anything else you'd better include me in on it, because otherwise the first time you cause trouble here or touch your gun, I'll be across the fence from you."

The old man sat like stone. "All respectfully," he coldly said. "You've got your job to do and we have ours. That's the long and short of it, Constable Bond." The old man stood up looking downward from his rangy height. "Twice now you've warned me, and both times you been within a hundred feet of this building. I don't think you'll find the men we want so close by, so you look your way and we'll look ours." Old Ezra turned and walked on out the roadside door. Jubal arose and also started on out. Bond called him softly by name.

"Don't let that old devil start anything, young man. Not in this town."

Jubal turned and walked on out thinking that his father and that stocky, muscular constable were like flint on steel. If he and old Ezra stayed on here, there was going to be trouble between them.

They went on up to the liverybarn and hung back for over an hour until Cullen's business slackened off sufficiently for his two hired men to care for it, then the old man buttonholed the Kentuckian and introduced himself. At once the ugly Kentuckian's little eyes turned sharp as daggers, and knowing. But he smiled when he

47

said in his slow drawl, "Tell me, Mister Braden—you a Southerner too?"

"I am," stated the old man. "And if you're interested the way I take you to be, Sir, I was a captain of the Sixteenth Virginia Cavalry, Confederate States Army."

Cullen's little eyes turned wickedly smiling. "Yeah," he drawled softly. "Well now, Mister Braden—me—I was with the Second Kentucky, a loyal outfit. A U.S. outfit."

The old man's expression froze for as long as he and the bitterly grinning lanky Kentuckian held their long, fixed stare. Then the old man said, a trifle stiffly Jubal thought, "It was a long time ago, Mister Cullen, and whatever a man believed then he can never entirely forfeit, but we used to sing a song in those days that is apt enough now. It was a thing called *Lorena,* and the words went: 'the years roll slowly by, Lorena'."

Cullen lifted his long upper lip to expose big square teeth. "Sure enough," he murmured. "The years have done rolled by sure enough, gents." Then Cullen turned brisk. "What was it you come in here for; horses, buggies, harness?"

"Information, Mister Cullen," Ezra said, still, Jubal thought, a little stiff-backed towards the rangy Kentuckian. "A few days back some men rode over the southward hills where we run cattle on the high desert, shot and killed my youngest. There were three of them."

Cullen's eyes became gradually veiled, his expression blanked over showing nothing. Jubal, watching closely, thought there was something darkly moving in the depths of Cullen's hooded eyes but he failed to define it.

"I'm right sorry to hear about your boy," Cullen said softly. "It's a rough and lawless land, my friend. Until Walt Bond came along we had no real law here. He was

48

in a couple hours back askin' about the same three. I can only tell you what I told him: Nothin'. I don't recall any three strangers ridin' together."

"Not strangers," said the old man. "They came from this settlement, Mister Cullen, and they rode back to it—afterwards."

"I see. You tracked 'em?"

"Yes, Sir."

"But you never seen 'em?"

"No, Sir."

Now the old man said something he hadn't mentioned before and which surprised Jubal. He said, "Mister Cullen; one of those men was riding a seal-brown horse. Another was riding a sorrel."

Cullen's gaze brightened briefly, so briefly that Jubal wasn't sure he'd caught that quick little flash at all. "Lots of seal-browns and sorrels around," he murmured to the old man. "In fact I've got at least five of each right here in my barn, but I haven't rented 'em to any three fellers hangin' together like you describe."

The old man seemed to harden his spirit towards the Kentuckian. For another moment he kept gazing upon Cullen, then he abruptly made a brusque little nod turned on his heel and walked back out of the barn. Jubal trailed after; he turned once, in the doorway, to look back. Cullen was intently watching the old man and Jubal could readily enough read his expression now—strong disapproval.

Without a word the old man hiked on out into the busy roadway. He was so absorbed with some thought that a buggy nearly ran him down. Jubal yanked his arm to drag the old man swiftly back out of harm's way, and afterwards, as they gained the opposite sidewalk in front of a bakery which stood midway between Redmond's

49

saloon and the boardinghouse, the old man said, "Jubal; he wouldn't help if he could. He was a fringe-stater; they were the worst of all."

Jubal paid no great attention to this; to him the war was something vague and long ago. He wasn't willing to believe these old men still lived it as fiercely as Ezra thought; too many years had passed, too many new lands had opened up. When he finally spoke it was something altogether different.

"How do you know one rode a sorrel and one a brown?"

"There was hair in the brush where they waited eastward from the house, son."

"Why didn't you tell that to the constable?"

Old Ezra didn't answer, he just shrugged. He was ranging a narrowed look up and down the tie racks.

7

IT WAS TWO O'CLOCK WHEN JUBAL RETURNED TO *Redmond's Saloon.* The old man wasn't with him, he had an aversion to saloons so he said he'd wander through town looking and listening.

The place wasn't quite as crowded at two as it had been at noon but there were still two dozen colorful frontiersmen there, mostly along the bar. They generally seemed to know one another, which wasn't unusual in an insular place such as isolated Jefferson.

Jubal bought another glass of that tepid beer and toyed with it. On his left stood that bronzed man with the little crescent scar beside his upper lip Jubal had noticed earlier. On his right was a nondescript cowboy who was both strong-smelling and troublesome looking.

50

Jubal kept his eye upon Amos Redmond. The notion persisted with him that if anyone could help in this settlement it would be either Redmond or Cullen. He lifted the glass to sip it. The man on his right bumped Jubal's elbow. It was a near thing but Jubal managed not to spill the beer. He looked around. The unkempt cowboy was gazing dead ahead as though unconscious of what he'd done. Jubal said nothing. The scar-faced man on his left turned and hailed a long-legged lean rider who'd just entered the barroom. Jubal studied this fresh stranger with mild interest. He was young and hatchet-faced, wore his gun on the left side instead of the right side, and walked with the rolling gait of a lifelong horseman. He smiled across at the scar-faced man and cruised over to join him.

Jubal lifted the glass again, and again his elbow was bumped. This time a little of the beer splashed upon Redmond's bartop, but Jubal didn't look around. It dawned slowly on him that the man on his right hadn't accidentally done that either time. But he couldn't prove this was so; the man kept staring straight ahead, his shoulders hunched, his body loosely upright as he leaned with both arms hooked upon the bar.

Jubal pretended to lift the glass the third time, stopped suddenly and watched the cowboy's right arm surreptitiously move upwards to jar him. He put the glass down, twisted slightly and said, "Slim; you just stand there now and take things easy like a good feller."

The cowboy kept staring bleakly ahead. He gave no indication that he'd heard. Jubal reached for his glass again. That arm moved slightly to bump him. Jubal turned half towards the unkempt, troublesome man. He thought the cowboy had been drinking; he studied him closely. The man was nearly Jubal's own height but he

51

lacked a good fifty pounds of being as heavy. His features were coarse and lined with hard living.

"Now listen, Slim, if you're joshin' let's just leave it like it is. What say?"

The cowboy didn't move a muscle or bat an eye. Jubal could as well have been talking to the wall. He knew what the stranger was doing, or thought he did anyway. It wasn't the first time a nettlesome drinker in a barroom deliberately annoyed another drinker. He reached for his glass, saw that moving arm, caught the lanky cowboy by the arm, flung him around and brought up a knotty big fist from down near his belt which connected solidly. The cowboy's head went violently backwards, he rose up nearly six inches off the floor and went backwards in a graceful dive that landed him squarely in the middle of a green, cloth-covered card table where four men were sitting relaxed playing poker. The table went over taking one of those card-players with it. This thoroughly astonished cow-man let out a squawk as table, cards, chips, money, and the knocked-out dead-weight of the stranger piled up on him. The other three men sprang clear but one stumbled and fell, got instantly back to his feet and glared in bewilderment around.

Amos Redmond, at the far side of the room, did not at once comprehend. When that man squawked though, he spun and started over. The barroom became hushed in a twinkling.

Evidently no one had actually seen what had happened but it required no vast powers of observation to see how hard that motionless, sprawling cowboy had been hit. There was a steady claret trickle past his slack lips where he'd evidently bitten through his tongue.

Jubal took two sideward steps and turned with his

52

mighty shoulders pressing against a wall. He waited and watched. That man with the little crescent-shaped scar was gazing dispassionately at the crumpled man amid the wreckage of that poker game. At his side stood that other one, the youthful, long-legged, left-handed man. He too was staring, but his face showed amazement.

Redmond stopped, looked over the upturned table and rolled his scar tissue eyebrows together when he brought his cold gaze on around to Jubal.

"Why?" he demanded, and added nothing to it.

"Maybe I shouldn't have," drawled big Jubal, regarding Redmond quietly. "He was pushin' for trouble, kept it up even after I asked him to leave be. So I put him to sleep."

One of the discomfited card players straightened up from examining the unconscious man. "You sure did," he muttered. "What'd you hit him with anyway; a sledgehammer?" This man shook his head at Amos Redmond. "If his damned neck ain't broke it'll be a miracle."

Redmond stood there on the edge of a decision glaring downward. "Two straight shots an' he figures he can clean out the house." He turned to the man with the little crescent scar. "Jack, he's one of yours; how about luggin' him out of here?"

Jack shrugged, looked at his left-handed companion and stepped around. The two of them caught hold of their limp acquaintance and proceeded on out through the crowd, out through the roadside doors, and disappeared.

Redmond paced up to Jubal, considered him for a moment with sharp words dammed up behind his teeth, then let off a big breath and turned as though to walk away. All he said was, "Stranger the next time just give me the high-sign. I don't like fights in here. Too much

53

furniture gets busted and it's damned hard to replace. Anyway, I got an oaken fellow behind the bar along with a bung-starter. Just give me the high-sign."

Redmond walked off, stiff-backed but unwilling to pursue the discussion further because, obviously, he had known the troublesome cowboy.

Behind Jubal those poker players helped their friend back to his feet, brushed him off and stood their table up again. Without a word they picked up everything off the floor, divided the chips, took their seats once more and one of them began laboriously counting the card deck. As he was doing this one of those men, an older, rugged-looking, compactly put together cattleman slowly turned and deliberately put a long, assessing gaze upon Jubal. This man slowly waggled his head back and forth, straightened back around and said evenly, "Whose pot was that, anyway?"

Gradually the saloon returned to normal but careful glances ran on down the bar to Jubal from time to time, sentences dwindled in mid-breath as these settlement men thoughtfully viewed Jubal's shoulders, powerful arms, calm features and trail-worn appearance. Clearly, behind his back, Jubal was going to hereafter be a center of interested conversation in Jefferson.

He never did drink that beer, and a little later as he headed down towards the boardinghouse, Constable Bond intercepted him. Bond looked displeased.

"I reckon I read off the wrong one of you," he told Jubal. "I had it figured the old man would be the troublesome one."

"Listen, Constable, I was mindin' my own business."

"Why of course you were, Mister Braden. They *all* are mindin' their own business when someone walks up out of a clear blue sky and picks a fight."

54

Jubal gazed down at the shorter but equally as broad constable. "Believe what you like," he murmured, and started past.

"Braden! I wasn't joshin' this morning about startin' trouble here. This is your last warning."

"I didn't start any trouble. I never saw that cowboy before in my life. I let the first couple of passes go by. The last time though, I didn't. You wouldn't have and neither would anyone else."

"Who was he, Braden?"

"I just told you—I never saw him before in my life. The only thing I know is that Amos Redmond said he was a friend of a dark-lookin' feller with a little odd-shaped scar at the outer edge of his upper lip. Redmond told that man and a skinny tall cowboy with him to lug the other one out of the saloon."

"Miles?" said Constable Bond, lifting his voice to make a question of that name. "The scar-faced feller—was he Jack Miles?"

Jubal lifted both shoulders and dropped them. "I'm fresh to the settlement, Constable. They all look pretty much alike to me."

Bond stood with sidewalk traffic breaking southward around him. He considered Jubal for a long moment, then broke his silence with: "I'd like to give you some advice. Gather up your paw and light out of here."

"You know we're not about to do that, Constable. You know why not, too."

"I'll find your brother's murderers, but if you two hang around there's going to be more trouble. I can feel it in my bones. That man you knocked out—his name's Bernie Sutton. He's mean, Mister Braden, and he's capable. He won't forget what you did to him. He and Jack Miles are old friends. They have other friends in

55

town too. That's why I gave you that advice. Go get your old man, saddle up and ride on back where you came from. Like I said—I'll find the men who shot your brother."

"I reckon not, Constable," said Jubal, and turned to walk away.

"If you don't," called Bond after him. "There's a good chance you'll join your brother!"

Jubal kept on walking.

Old Ezra was in their room at the boardinghouse. He had bathed, put on the fresh, rumpled shirt he'd brought along in his saddlebag and he'd even trimmed his beard. But his mane of stiff standing grizzled gray hair stood awry as always and after he'd listened to Jubal's tale of the encounter at *Redmond's Saloon,* his fierce, greeny old eyes lit up with a steady wild fire.

"I could've told you, boy," he rumbled. "There's nothing but evil and iniquity in those places with their vicious men and painted women. No self-respectin' man should ever take his whisky in a saloon, he should take it by his own campfire or in the decent privacy of his own house. Now tell me—this man you struck—what did he look like?"

Jubal shrugged. His recollection of Bernie Sutton was vague for the basic reason that Bernie Sutton was vague. "Dirty," he said. "Unwashed, a mite shorter'n I am. Some lighter in heft. Mean actin'. That's about the size of him, Paw."

"And this Jack Miles—what of him?"

"Looked to be cut from the same cloth, only a mite cleaner. He's got a little moon-shaped scar alongside his upper lip.

"The same," muttered the old man so quietly it seemed he was mumbling to himself. "The same man."

56

"What?"

The old man raised his shaggy face. "That constable —he said when you want information you ask merchants. Well; I don't think much of Walter Bond. He sits over at that jailhouse too much. I walked down through the shacks south of town, Jubal, and I asked questions. A woman and two men recollect seein' three fellers ride into Jefferson about midday some few days back. They didn't know their names but each said they'd seen these men around town often enough. One had that little scar alongside his mouth you just now described." Old Ezra squeezed his eyes nearly closed and dropped his voice. "Jack Miles, Jubal. Him and this Bernie Sutton and one other. I think, boy, we've found our cold blooded murderers."

Jubal strode across to a grimy window, lifted it and gazed downwards into the dusty, sunlighted hot roadway. "The other one's tall and thin and young. I never caught his name but he was in there with Miles. It was him helped Miles carry Sutton out of the saloon afterwards. He's younger'n the others and wears a gun on the left side."

The old man came over to also stand gazing downward. His bloodless, slash of a mouth was cruelly curved upwards at its outer corners. He considered the jailhouse where men were working out the back, and he said, "That constable couldn't find his hip pockets with both hands. We've been in this place not quite one full day an' already we know all we've got to know."

Jubal shook his head. "We've got to be more certain than this, Paw. Did you check to see what color horses Miles and those other two ride?"

"No. We'll do that now. Come along."

"Come along where?"

Ezra picked up his shapeless old hat, dropped it atop his shaggy head and looked annoyedly over at his son. "Why, the liverybarn to start with, an' if we get nothing from that big-nosed fringe-stater named Cullen, we'll look elsewhere. But one thing's certain, Jubal; folks'll know what color horses those three ride."

They left the room, went downstairs and out into the afternoon coolness. Among the passersby were men who, recognising Jubal, looked, and looked again, as they paced on by. Over at the liverybarn several men were standing in a little puddle of useless shade talking. One of those men was Wilford Cullen. Another was that youthful, left-handed cowboy who'd been in Redmond's place with Jack Miles.

Jubal pointed this man out to old Ezra as the pair of them started on across through roadway dust towards the barn. They were in mid-roadway when a little red-wheeled runabout came hastening along behind a sleek, high-headed big chestnut mare. Jubal paused to allow this rig to run on by and heard someone softly speak his name. He looked up. The constable's lovely daughter was driving. She threw Jubal a flashing smile then whipped on by.

Old Ezra, his full attention upon those idly talking men across in front of the barn, missed this brief scene. He stepped out after the rig went past with his long, thrusting stride, his expression grim and forbidding.

8

WILFORD CULLEN SAW THEM COMING WHILE THEY were still half across the road. He looked, then he said something sharp from the corner of his mouth. Both the men standing with Cullen turned and looked. Jubal, watching the youthful, lean and left-handed man, saw his eyes widen slightly at sight of the old man walking a foot or two ahead of Jubal.

The old man stepped up, gazed straight at the rangy Kentuckian and gravely nodded. "Mister Cullen," he said evenly, "my boy ran into a man in that saloon across the way and they had a slight disagreement."

The left-handed man faintly snorted bringing old Ezra's glance over to him. "Slight disagreement," said the youthful cowboy, "don't quite cover it, oldtimer. That feller's neck bones are dislocated. Your son liked to took his head plumb off his neck."

"That, sir," intoned the old man, "is the risk a man runs when he goes huntin' trouble."

The left-handed cowboy dropped his eyes and shrugged. Wilford Cullen, eyeing Jubal with his small, shrewd eyes, said, "Plumb right, Mister Braden. You're plumb right. What can I do for you?"

"Step into the barn."

Cullen turned away from his companions. The three of them went well beyond earshot where rank shade lay, and stopped. "Now, Mister Cullen," stated the old man, "I want to know what color horse that man rode that Jubal knocked down."

"Sutton?" said Cullen. "Why, he rides a bay horse, Mister Braden."

"I see. And his friend out there with the left-hand gun; what color horse does he ride, sir?"

"That's Mike Leary. He rides a gray horse, Mister Braden."

"And Jack Miles, Sir?"

"Well; Jack rides a dark chestnut sorrel," stated Cullen, his little eyes watching the old man with sudden, sharp interest. "You wasn't figurin' those three might be the ones you're lookin' for were you, Mister Braden, because I can tell you it isn't at all likely."

Old Ezra stood quietly. Jubal knew how the old man felt. He'd been so sure, over at the boardinghouse, and now that certainty had been swept away by Cullen's description of those three horses. Jubal turned and stood gazing out into the roadway. They were right back where they'd started from, but with one difference, they were no longer strangers in Jefferson. Not after his run-in with Bernie Sutton over at Amos Redmond's place.

Across the road Mike Leary, the left-handed man, strolled along towards Redmond's tie rack with that same man he and Cullen had been talking to out front. Jubal watched those two. When they came even with the rack the other cowboy threw Leary a careless little wave and sauntered on towards the saloon's doors while Mike Leary paced on around behind some tied horses over there, squeezed in beside one blocky animal, unlooped his reins, backed the animal out and stepped up over leather, settled himself and gave the horse a little knee-pressure. The horse started immediately walking docilely northward. In color that horse wasn't gray as Wilford Cullen had said, he was sorrel.

Jubal casually turned back to gaze at the rawboned liveryman, to study him with fresh interest. Cullen had patently lied. Unless Leary was riding someone else's

60

animal, Cullen had deliberately lied about the color horse Leary rode, and that was interesting. But Jubal kept his silence. When the old man and Cullen finished talking Jubal walked back out onto the plankwalk with Ezra. Out there he said, "What do you think?" to the old man.

Ezra audibly sighed and shook his shaggy head. "I was so sure, son. So sure."

Jubal made a dry, blunt statement. "Cullen lied, Paw. Leary took a sorrel horse off Redmond's rack yonder and rode off on him. Sorrel—not gray. I saw them both; Leary and his sorrel horse."

Ezra gazed down his nose at big Jubal while rusty dark color turned his face splotchy. He started to swing completely around. Jubal caught his arm.

"Not yet," he said. "Stay clear of Cullen for a while. I'm going over to the saloon again. Someone over there's got some answers, I reckon. You leave Cullen alone until we're sure."

"All I want is to ask one question, son."

"No. I got an idea how that'll end. He doesn't care for you already. And Paw; if he deliberately lied to shield Leary he had his good enough reasons. You go back in there and stir him up an' he'll pass the word to Leary we're getting close."

"Well . . . ?"

"This is their town, Paw, and nighttime's coming on. It'd be right easy for any one of them to stand between two buildings and pick us off like they did John."

Ezra said: "I'll be waitin' over at the boarding house, Jubal," and started back across the road.

Wilford Cullen came strolling forth from his gloomy liverybarn. He paused amiably beside Jubal and gazed out where old Ezra was moving across through roadway dust.

"It'd be right hard on a man to lose a boy like your pappy did, Mister Braden," he said easily. "But he's barkin' up the wrong tree this time."

"How's that?" asked Jubal, eyeing the ugly Kentuckian.

"Oh; askin' about Bernie Sutton'n Mike Leary an' Jack Miles."

"I don't recollect him askin' specifically about those three, Mister Cullen."

The liveryman turned his head, studied Jubal's face a moment, then shrugged. "Sure not," he murmured. "I reckon it just looked that way to me. Well; 'hope you find those killers, Mister Braden."

Cullen turned and went back down into the strong-smelling dark runway of his liverybarn where two hostlers were busily caring for two wagons which had come just turned in.

Jubal moved off in the direction of *Redmond's Saloon,* got almost to the doors and was fetched up short by Constable Bond. The barrel-shaped lawman was chewing a toothpick. His expression was speculative as he gazed up into Jubal's bronzed face.

"Not goin' back in there so soon, are you?" he inquired.

Jubal nodded and reached ahead to push back a door. Bond swung and said, "I'll go with you." He stayed with Jubal right on up to the bar where men gave way on either side to make room.

As usual, Redmond's place was crowded. It was now near enough to evening for the saloon to have its early, nightly celebrants. From the corner of his eye Jubal saw men speak briefly back and forth and nod over in his direction. The men who'd seen him knock out Bernie Sutton were passing word among the new arrivals who he was and what he'd done.

62

Amos Redmond walked down his bar, put a look of mild disapproval upon Jubal, then leaned across from Walter Bond. "What'll it be?" he asked, and before Bond could reply Jubal spoke up.

"That Sutton feller I had the little argument with, Mister Redmond. How well do you know him?"

Amos turned and kept his mild look of disapproval. "Why?" he challenged. "Aren't you satisfied, cowboy?"

Constable Bond broke in to say, "Amos; this here is Jubal Braden. He's the brother of that young feller who got killed over the mountains that I was tellin' you about earlier."

Redmond's frown didn't entirely depart, but he looked upon Jubal with a fresh expression of interest. "I see. Well, in answer to your question, Mister Braden: I know Bernie Sutton as well as Walt Bond does, I reckon."

"Is he troublesome?" Jubal asked.

Redmond inclined his head incisively. "He is, Sir. That's why I didn't say more to you than I did today. Bernie's mean an' he's troublesome. Even when he's stone-sober he's not a pleasant feller to be around. To be perfectly honest—I was glad you belted him, because if you hadn't I figured I was going to have to sooner or later. He was goin' around like a bear with a sore behind all day; mostly, the fellers he'd been chousin' walked away. You didn't." Redmond lifted his thick shoulders and dropped them.

"What color horse does he ride, Mister Redmond?"

Walter Bond's head came swiftly around; it was as though something had just struck Bond with solid impact. Bond said, "Bernie rides a dappled gray, Mister Braden, but his running mate Leary rides a sorrel and Jack Miles rides a big seal-brown."

63

Amos Redmond, who evidently knew Constable Bond quite well, rolled his brows together now as he looked at the lawman. "What's this all about, Walt?" he asked. "Are those three maybe mixed up in this killing over the mountains?"

Bond and Jubal steadily regarded one another for some little time before the constable answered Redmond. "It's beginning to smell a little like they *could've* had a hand in it, Amos. At least it won't hurt to ask a few questions."

"Before you do that, Constable," said Jubal quietly, "explain to me why Will Cullen over at the liverybarn deliberately lied to my paw an' me a little while ago."

Jubal explained about Cullen's falsehood regarding the color horse Mike Leary rode. Amos Redmond and Walter Bond exchanged a long look at one another which didn't get by Jubal. Redmond said gruffly, "Mister Braden, you're skirtin' around some dangerous men. If I was in your boots I'd step mighty easy here. Will Cullen's no fool."

Jubal turned wry. "I didn't have him pegged for a fool from the first time I saw him, Mister Redmond, but that's not my main concern right now. What I want to know is why he lied to me like that?"

"Well; Cullen and Jack Miles are sort of pardners in some of their deals around town."

"Deals?"

Walter Bond hooked one booted foot upon Redmond's brass rail, leaned back and spoke carefully, as though he was selecting each word with considerable care.

"Miles puts up money from time to time. He and Cullen buy land and resell it to emigrants. They also buy and sell livestock and other things; surplus loadings, for example, from wagon trains leaving Oregon southbound for California. They sometimes do a good business. This time of year especially, when folks who are leaving Oregon, make up their wagon trains."

Jubal listened to all this, found nothing wrong with it, and said, "Tell me, Constable: Just what does Jack Miles do for a living, aside from these deals of his?"

Bond lifted his eyes to Amos Redmond again, and shrugged. "He has a section of land northeastward, Mister Braden. But mostly he uses it for fattening up the foot-sore and tired critters he buys from emigrant trains. He doesn't ranch much; turns cattle loose in the hills sometimes, when he buys a herd off some desperate emigrant. Leary and Sutton ride for him." Bond threw up his hands. "Every town has its Jack Miles, Mister Braden. They capitalize off the misery and poor luck of others. But it's not against the law. It's simply business."

"Their work could take them away from Jefferson for days at a time, couldn't it, Constable?"

Bond grudgingly nodded. "It could. In fact, it often enough does."

"So," pressed on Jubal. "The three of them could be gone say two or three days and no one'd pay any attention."

"Well yes. But that's no proof they killed your brother over the mountains, Mister Braden."

Jubal straightened up off the bar. "It's no proof they *didn't* kill him, either, Constable."

Amos Redmond, who had, through this exchange between Bond and Braden, been engrossed in a careful study of the back of one hand, said slowly, "Walt; they're not above it. You know that as well as I do. You recollect the rumors last fall about those gold prospectors who upped and disappeared over near Des Chutes, and how their animals showed up here last winter over in Will Cullen's trading corral."

Bond seemed a little uncomfortable when he said, "I recollect that, sure. But at the time Will told me he'd bought the critters from some passing Injuns."

"That's possible of course," murmured Amos Redmond, in a tone that left no doubt at all in his hearers' minds that he wasn't at all convinced this was the truth.

Constable Bond drew up off Redmond's bar. "I'll talk with Jack," he said. Then he turned on Jubal. "About the color of those horses, Mister Braden: If you'n your paw knew this before, why did you withhold it from me when we talked earlier?"

Jubal shrugged. "I didn't know. My paw knew, and that's his way, Constable."

"Well dammit; what else do you fellers know?"

"Nothing, to my knowledge, Constable. Nothing at all."

Bond stared hard at Jubal before he abruptly turned. "I think I'd better go have a talk with your paw before I have that talk with Jack Miles, doggone it all. I don't like your paw's way of keeping things back."

Jubal said nothing. Constable Bond turned and strode out through the crowded room to the yonder roadway. Behind, watching his departure, rugged Amos Redmond said to Jubal, "I'd keep a sharp watch, Mister Braden. Real sharp. Walt Bond's a good man for his job, but he's only one man, an' by now, if Jack Miles and the others *are* mixed up in this murder, they'll surely know you an' your paw are hunting for them. I've seen more'n one man shot in the back around Jefferson."

"We'll look out," murmured Jubal. "One more

66

question, Mister Redmond. If Miles killed my brother, is it likely Cullen would know that?"

"I'd say he'd know, Mister Braden. They're a lot closer'n most folks know. In my occupation I get to know pretty much how the wind blows in Jefferson. I'd say offhand that Will Cullen would know; I'd also say that's why he lied to you a while back." Redmond raised his steely eyes. "To give Jack time enough to understand you're after him, and to make plans to take care of that."

"I'm obliged," said Jubal quietly.

Redmond looked sardonic. "I didn't do you any favors, Mister Braden. None at all. You an' your paw are up against Miles, Leary, and Bernie Sutton: Three of the fastest guns in Jefferson."

Redmond turned and walked away.

9

THEY HAD THEIR SUPPER AT THE LITTLE BEANERY IN total silence. Afterwards they returned to their room at the boardinghouse. Here, they talked; here, the old man asked questions of Jubal until the whole idea of Miles's culpability was straight in his mind. Then he fished for his stubby pipe, filled it and lit up as he sat over there before the window in their darkened room, and he rocked forth and back, his thoughts turning his face alternately cruel and thoughtful, merciless and sly. He was planning. A man whose resolve had remained ironlike for seven decades, and whose resourcefulness had been proven adequate through a thousand dilemmas, was no one to take lightly, particularly when, as now, every fiber of his being was concentrated

67

wholly upon what must be done in young John's name.

He didn't hear Jubal leave. He puffed and rocked and forged his schemes for vengeance, and he was now more than ever like some ancient patriarch swollen with a coldness and a wrathfulness against the enemies of his breed. He sat there for hours, until the town's lights flickered out one by one, brooding on the mystery of his days, the insoluble problems of love and hatred, the foulness which had been perpetrated against his youngest who had been too gentle, too kindly to see young animals mangled and tortured at the marking grounds. A dozen agonizing memories rose to haunt him, to twist his thoughts first one way then another, to plague his spirit and feed the low, steady flames of his will to repay those who had done this to his youngest, and in the end he took up his Winchester and stole out of the room, stole down through the boardinghouse's empty little parlor and crossed over to go around the back of Cullen's barn and slip in over there to rig out his horse, lead it silently out under the cobalt sky, mount it and strike off northeasterly.

He knew the way to Jack Miles's place. He had a way of secretiveness about him that until today Jubal hadn't encountered; no man lives to his seventieth year without developing a secret nature, something which he keeps close by and hidden from others. He'd made inquiries about Jack Miles and his section of fenced-off land four miles off from town. He'd also asked about Leary and Bernie Sutton, and in rougher language than Jubal had heard from Amos Redmond and Walt Bond, the old man had got about the same analysis of those three. He'd heard little against Wilford Cullen though. It appeared that folks didn't generally know Cullen and Miles were partners. But that didn't trouble the old man

68

now, as he rode off through the calm night with a Winchester balanced across his legs. He had it in mind to seek out Cullen later, and also to take care of Bernie Sutton who was lying with his neck in plaster-of-paris over in the doctor's residence. He'd appear to confront those two later.

The night was hushed, far back a steady glow here and there showed where Jefferson lay, out there upon the Oregon prairie. Farther off, softly luminous under silvery starshine, were visible the southward mountain-ramparts and lonely peaks. His youngest lay down across those spiny ridges cold in his dark, dark grave.

When he thought he was about close enough the old man left his horse ground-hitched and struck out on foot, a big, rawboned and gaunt old wraith wise in the ways of fading out in darkness, wise in the ways of lethal stalking, his bearded old face tilted upwards just enough for pale pewter light to show its rock-set jaw and its wild, savage old greeny eyes.

There was no light in the yonder rough buildings when he first sighted them, which he liked, and there was a drowsy quiet up there too, which kept him gliding along until, within shooting distance, he paused to lightly drop to one knee and make his careful appraisal on ahead.

Miles and Leary would be sleeping over there, one in the thick-walled, low and ugly log house, the other in the smaller, equally as ugly and functional log bunk-house which lay easterly of Miles's sod-roofed log barn.

He wished he'd brought along a skinning knife. This wasn't work for a gun. A few low words at bedside to let those two know who was there in the darkness with them, a slash and a plunge—twice—then the gushing of dark blood, something to wash away sin and grief in a ritualistic manner.

But he had no knife. He had only his Winchester and that old rebored Dragoon revolver. They would have to do; they would of course be adequate.

He made his noiseless way right up to the corner of Miles's barn. From there he had a good, gloomy view of everything roundabout; the bunkhouse, which was closest, and over yonder the main house. Two horses in a pole corral softly snorted at his scent and stood back stiff-legged to roll their eyes when he loomed up silently to study them for a moment before passing the barn's full length to emerge where he had only a little starlighted distance to cross through before reaching the bunkhouse. One of those horses made a snort at his wraithlike passing along.

From inside the barn another horse rustled bedding and dragged a tie-chain gratingly across a manger. This brought the old man to a quick halt out there. He gazed backwards at those two loose animals. They appeared to be saddle animals, not team horses, but in the closeness of full night it was hard to be sure of that.

There was no reason why a third animal shouldn't be tethered in the barn even though only Miles and Leary were here. Often enough cattlemen kept one horse tied inside especially if they happened to own a stallion. Still, when a man is stalking other men, it pays to make sure of things before passing them on by.

The old man straightened up and slipped along the barn's front wall as far as the doorless maw of the building. He could hear that tethered animal in there restlessly moving, evidently roused from its rest by the soft snorting of the horse yonder in the corral. He craned for an inward look, saw nothing because of the total blackness, stepped in and, holding his Winchester

70

low and ready in both hands, paced over in the direction of those little restless sounds.

He found the tied animal without any great trouble, but he also found something else. This horse was *saddled!* In the middle of the night without a light showing anywhere, here stood a saddled horse with its bridle hanging from the horn. No one could forget to off-saddle. He brought his bushy brows together in wonderment. He stepped in closer, reached out one-handed and felt the mouthpiece of that hanging bit. It was still wet! His hand recoiled from that warm, damp steel as though it had encountered a coiled snake; he started to whip around. It was his intention to get out of that barn as swiftly as he could, for obviously there was something not quite right around here. But he didn't quite complete his turn.

"Steady you damned old devil you! Don't make another move or I'll sure 'nough splatter your innards all over the wall!"

The old man knew that voice at once. There were certain mannerisms of speech which came only out of the Deep South. And that voice fairly dripped with rancor; the same rancor, only stronger now and undisguised, which Cullen had shown towards Ezra at their other meetings.

"You skulkin' old reprobate drop that Winchester. Thought you had it all figured out didn't you, Braden, damn your lousy soul. Well; you weren't the only one who's been doin' some figurin'. I said *drop that gun!"*

Ezra stood awkwardly twisted and stiff. "Cullen, where are you?" he asked softly. "Show yourself, man."

"You drop that Winchester, Braden, or I'll kill you sure 'nough."

There was no mistaking the promise inherent in that

71

threat. The old man let his Winchester fall and strike the packed earth floor of Jack Miles's barn.

"Cullen; come out," he said again, straining for movement in the thick layered darkness.

Cullen ignored that. He said, "Now the pistol, you old devil. Let it drop too. An' if you try anythin' cute I'll gut shoot you five times before you can even figure out where I'm firin' from. Now drop it!"

"You listen, Cullen!"

"Listen nothing, Braden. You could've left things be, but no. You're one of those vengeful ones. I know the type, damn you. I ought to—I skewered my share of 'em after the war for resistin' federal edicts. You're just another one of 'em too. Now drop that damned pistol!"

From out the back a thin sounding voice spoke up. "Will; did you get him?"

"I got him, Jack," exulted Cullen. "He walked in here neat as a pin."

"You got him disarmed?"

"No. He's still got his pistol."

Miles's thin voice said, "Braden; shuck the pistol. You got the chance of a snowball in hell. Mike's out front, I'm back here, and Will Cullen's—."

"Shut up," squawked the liveryman swiftly. "Wait until he sheds his damned pistol. I don't trust this old devil."

Miles chuckled. It was an unnatural sound in the grim and lethal barn gloom. "Braden; shuck that pistol an' let's get this over with."

The old man's chagrin was monumental. Never before in his eventful life had he permitted himself to be boxed in by such a sorry crew. He drew out his revolver and hurled it away. "All right," he thundered at the three of them. "I'm unarmed. Now come and take me, you

72

scum!" He squared around facing towards the rear doorway. From behind him and overhead a man's heavy, spurred boots crunched down across the rungs of a loft ladder. Cullen had been above him, not out in the barn somewhere. He looked over, made out the rangy Kentuckian's form and said a fierce word.

Once again Jack Miles chuckled. He walked on up into the barn with a cocked, dead level six-gun in his right fist. From out front youthful Mike Leary also approached. Mike was also holding a cocked revolver, only he had his gun in his left hand.

They stopped close enough to see the old man. He faced them like a bear brought to bay, his head tilted, his nostrils flared, and his lipless mouth set in an ancient pattern of unflinching defiance.

"Scum," he growled. "Murderers. What did it get you? We had no cache. Why did you kill him? He was a boy. You could've held him under a gun."

Jack Miles said, "Yeah; and afterwards he could've identified each of us. Old man, turn and walk out there into the yard. Go easy now; try runnin' an' you'll never see another dawn."

They herded him along out into the cooling night where a belated moon was casting its watery light earthward. Out there he turned on them, his chagrin near to choking him. "Shoot!" he said, and cursed them. "For I can identify you two. Cullen; you're a sorry liar. Jubal and I figured out that you lied to us about the color horse Leary rode."

"Did you now?" asked Cullen softly, indifferently, his fist curling tighter around the gun-butt he held. "That's too bad, you old fool."

The old man threw out a big arm. "For nothing. You lied for nothing, Cullen. And you, Miles, you killed my

73

boy for nothing; you ransacked the place and got not one red cent for all your riding and your ransacking. And now, you filthy scum, you'll kill me for the same reward—nothing."

The old man hurled that last word at them at the same time he lunged for Miles. Cullen, springing wildly away, his face twisted with sudden fright, shrieked at Mike Leary, "Shoot, dammit shoot!"

But Leary dared not; Jack Miles was staggering backwards under the old man's roaring charge. A bullet sent into old Ezra would surely pass on through and also hit Miles.

Leary danced inward with his gun barrel raised up high. He struck old Ezra but the blow glanced off the skull and crunched into one bony old shoulder. Ezra caught hold of Miles's gun arm and hung on desperately as Leary, and now Will Cullen too, jumped in to beat at him with their pistols.

The old man suddenly became silent as those men behind him beat at him unmercifully with their pistols. Jack Miles had presence enough of mind to hurl his own six-gun away, out of the old man's reach. He closed with Ezra and although he was decades younger, the old man's ferocity swamped him.

Leary cursed and repeatedly struck downward with his gun. Old Ezra twisted this way and that to make those assailing steel barrels miss, and they often did, but the blows were coming now with savage ferocity; if he got away from one battering blow he ran into two more from a different direction. His mind reeled and his senses turned dull, but he still fought on seeking to get his powerful fingers around Jack Miles's throat.

Cullen whipped right behind the old man and swung a high strike. There was a fearful thud. Old Ezra did not

74

drop under it, he staggered crazily, his breath exploding outward. His eyes aimlessly turned in their sockets but he now had Jack Miles by the gullet and was hanging on with a wildness. Cullen's gun barrel smashed down again and again. Ultimately the old man slumped, dropped both his arms and lay still in a twisted heap.

"God," whispered Jack Miles, putting forth a hand to steady himself. "God." He had his other hand up to his throat. "Kill him," he croaked. "Kill that damned dirty old . . ."

Cullen stepped over athwart the old man, one big leg planted on either side of his slack body, raised his gun barrel and rolled with his entire weight behind that blow. He did this three times, each time hitting Ezra on the head. Then he stepped clear and glared downward, breathing hard.

He called Ezra a sizzling name and through panting breaks in his loud breathing, said, "That'll learn him, damn his lousy soul anyway. That'll learn him."

It was young Mike Leary who made the bent over final inspection and who afterwards straightened up, holstered his .45 and quietly said to Jack Miles, "We got to find where he left his horse, lash him to it and turn the horse loose. Can't have him found anywhere around the ranch, Jack."

Miles was sucking in big sweeping breaths of air. "Is he done for?" he asked.

Leary nodded. "Dead," he muttered. "Look at his head; it's all busted out of shape."

Jack Miles stepped over and peered downward. He was still holding his throat with one hand where the old man's talon-like fingers had ground hard into his flesh.

"He's a devil," muttered Miles. "I didn't like his looks the first time I laid eyes on him."

75

"Yeah," agreed hard breathing Wilford Cullen, "an' if I hadn't ridden out here tonight to warn you, Jack, he'd have gotten the pair of you sure."

Leary was examining his pistol barrel without heeding the old man or his companions. "Think I bent it," he mumbled. "Damned old coot had a skull of cast iron."

Miles looked around at Cullen. "You're right," he said. "Good thing we figured one of 'em might try something like this and got ready for 'em. But what of the younger one; he might be sneakin' around too."

Cullen was doubtful. "Naw; if he was he'd have come a-shootin' while we were beatin' on the old man. Naw; that other one was still in town when I rode out. I saw him standin' near the general store talkin' to Walt Bond."

The mention of Constable Bond's name brought Jack Miles back to normal. He dropped his hand and said, "Mike; go find his horse and fetch it back here." As Leary nodded and strode off Miles turned on Cullen. "You get back to town. Have a drink or two at Redmond's. Let folks see you, if there are still any folks up this late."

"What about your alibi, Jack?"

"Never mind. After we get rid of the body we'll think of something."

10

JUBAL LISTENED TO CONSTABLE BOND WHILE HIS thoughts were elsewhere. He hadn't seen the old man leave the boardinghouse for the simple reason that he'd been walking the darkened byways breathing deeply of the cool night air.

"If he isn't in your room," Bond was saying, "where would he be? I wanted to talk to him, Jubal. I want to see him before I ride out in the morning and talk to Jack Miles."

"If you'd tried earlier, Constable, he'd have been handy. Now—I don't know where—he went."

"But you can guess," said Bond dryly. "Go get your horse and the pair of us'll take a little ride."

"Where to?"

Bond grimaced. "Out to the Miles place, where else?"

Jubal considered. It was late and he'd had an arduous day. He wasn't at all convinced the old man would try bracing Miles and Leary alone, so he didn't view a long ride this late at night favorably.

Bond said: "Go on, boy. Take my word for it, your paw's up to no good."

"You're sure of that, are you, Constable?"

"Well," Bond quietly replied, "there are two carbine-boots behind the door at your boardinghouse room. One has a Winchester in it and the other boot is plumb empty. Now that rifle up there, I figure, belongs to you. The empty one belongs to your father. His scabbard is empty, Jubal; what does that sound like to you?"

"I'll fetch my horse," said Jubal, and strode on across to the lamp-lighted doorway of Cullen's barn. But he didn't go at once after his mount, he instead sent the night hostler after the beast while he strolled up and down the tie-stalls looking for old Ezra's horse.

It wasn't there. Neither was the old man's saddle.

Jubal rode across to where Constable Bond was waiting astride a horse. He said, "I reckon you might be right at that, Constable. His outfit's gone from the barn."

They rode side by side on out of Jefferson and turned

77

eastward through the late night. A mile and a half along Walt Bond tipped back in the saddle, gazed at the serene overhead sky and said, "Jubal; there'd be blood on the moon tonight—if there was a moon. When you've been at my trade as long as I have, you get so's you can feel things."

They were a half-mile farther out when somewhere northward of them a ridden horse clattered past at a swift gait.

Jubal listened and cocked his head to make out the route of that invisible rider. "Towards Jefferson," he pronounced. "You reckon that might be Leary or Miles?"

Bond made no guess about this. "It could be anyone; maybe some tomfool cowboy headin' in for a drink before the saloon closes. Anyway, let him go; we're not hunting just anyone tonight."

They came finally within sight of the Miles place. Bond didn't hesitate. He rode straight along into the yard. Both the bunkhouse and the main house were totally dark. Bond, who appeared to know this yard well enough, reined off over by the barn where some tie-poles stood, swung down and made his horse secure.

While he waited for Jubal the lawman sniffed and looked. As Jubal came around he said, "Dust; I can taste it."

They strolled over to the main house, banged upon the door and waited. It was a middling-to-long wait, then Miles himself came out with a high-held lantern asking who it was and what they wanted this time of night. Bond asked if Jack had been visited by anyone this night. Miles lowered his lantern to see their faces, and from above and behind that protecting light answered up that no one had been around to his knowledge. He then asked whom the lawman was seeking.

"Old man Braden," responded Bond, his eyes studying Jack Miles. "He rode out of town a while back. We figured he might've come this way."

Miles snorted, rolled his eyes over to Jubal, and softly said, "Why should he come out here?"

Jubal threw back Miles's hard look as he answered up. "He had his reasons, Miles."

"Is that so? And just what might those reasons be?"

Walt Bond threw his voice between those two. "Jack; I'd like to know where you an' Mike and Bernie were three, four days ago, when you weren't around town."

"Hell, Walt," said Miles easily, "We were around town. We been around town for the last two, three weeks. If you didn't see us that doesn't prove we weren't there. What's this all about, anyway?"

"Murder," said Jubal. "A murder committed in cold blood down the far side of the southward mountains, Miles."

Miles stepped ahead to a porch railing, carefully balanced his lantern there, hitched at his beltless trousers and faced his visitors. He was shirtless and gunless. His hair was rumpled as though he'd been abed, but to Jubal's way of thinking, Miles's face and eyes showed total wakefulness; if he could come out of a deep, sound slumber looking as dry-eyed and unpuffy as he now looked, he was the only person Jubal had ever encountered who could. Jubal didn't believe Miles had been asleep at all.

"Is Mike over at the bunkhouse?" Walt Bond asked.

Miles shrugged. "Darned if I know; he went to town earlier for a few drinks. I don't know whether he got back yet or not. Go on over and see, Constable."

"Yeah, think I will, Jack. But tell me again—you haven't seen any sign of old man Braden tonight?"

"None at all, Bond."

"And you haven't had any visitors tonight?"

"No. If anyone came ridin' in they sure didn't waken me."

Bond stepped to the edge of the porch and when Jubal hung back watching Miles, Bond said gruffly, "Come along, Jubal. Let's ask Mike if he's seen or heard anything around here tonight."

They left Jack Miles standing out front and walked across the soft-lighted yard. When they were within a few feet of the dark bunkhouse Walter Bond turned and whispered: "Either he's the soundest sleeper in Oregon, or else he's a cussed liar. Dust doesn't hang this long in the air so's it can be smelled. Someone was here, and not too long ago either."

They entered the bunkhouse. Walt Bond lit a match and held it high. There were two rumpled bunks but the place was vacant. The match burnt down, warmed Bond's fingers and he dropped it, stepped on it, turned and went back outside. Jubal followed him. When they were back over by their horses Bond motioned for Jubal to mount up. Without a word they walked their horses side by side back the way they'd come. Behind them, Miles's house was totally blacked out again; elsewhere around the ranch buildings that same solid hush lay which their arrival had briefly broken.

"Nope," said Bond. "Jack wasn't tellin' the truth. That dust said someone'd been there not long before we rode in."

Jubal was riding along considering something in his right hand. He said nothing. Constable Bond lifted his

80

head to further test the air, but there was no scent or taste of dust out here so he settled back down in the saddle and turned his head.

Jubal met the constable's troubled gaze. "He had a caller," Jubal quietly stated. "My father."

"Huh? You don't know that to be a fact," exclaimed the burly lawman.

"Yes I do, Constable. But I didn't know it for a fact until I walked over to get on my horse." Jubal pushed out his left hand for Walt Bond to see what was lying upon his broad palm.

"A pipe," said Bond.

"Not *a* pipe, Constable; this is my father's pipe. I was there last winter when he carved it out of a burl. I'd know this pipe anywhere."

Bond halted his animal, looped his reins and took the little stubby, strong-smelling pipe for closer examination. Finally he looked up without speaking.

Jubal said: "Something else, Mister Bond. That bunk closest the door back there—a man had been sitting on it not too long before we rode in, so if Leary went to town as Miles said, then he either returned and sat down—probably to take off his boots—and left again suddenly, or else there's a third man staying at Miles's place we don't know about."

"Hell," said Walt Bond, passing back the little pipe. "Leary could've sat on his bunk this afternoon some time, or even this morning, for all we know."

Jubal shook his head. "It was still warm to the touch where he'd been sitting, Constable. When you walked back out of the bunkhouse I put my hand down there. The blankets were still warm."

Now Walter Bond's face smoothed out into a perfectly blank expression. He steadily regarded Jubal

81

for a long moment before he half twisted and looked back through the late night soft light towards those silhouetted buildings back there.

Jubal broke in upon Bond's speculative thoughts. "He was here and something happened to him. You ride along this way, back towards town, and I'll split off and ride northward for a while. If the old man got away from them and he's hurt, which I think might be the case, I want to find him. Whatever happened back there in that yard I want to know about."

Jubal reined off leaving Walter Bond still sitting his saddle looking increasingly troubled. He turned just once, that was when the constable called after him saying, "Wait. Let's think this over. It appears to me if Miles knows anything we should go back and ask him some questions."

Jubal shook his head while his horse kept right on walking. "The old man isn't at the ranch. The important thing right now is to find him. If he's hurt, and if Miles stalls us, the old man could die out here somewhere."

Bond didn't argue but he didn't seem to be convinced his way wasn't the best. Still, he rode back the way they'd come out to the Miles ranch and from time to time surveyed the onward countryside.

He lost sight of Jubal almost immediately after the larger and younger man cut straight northward. After that Bond passed through the same depthless silence he'd ridden through coming out here. He had the few lights of Jefferson in sight, small but persevering, when he began to wonder about that horseman they'd passed on the way out. He thought it likely now, that this rider had been Ezra Braden. This notion kept him occupied until he was within a half-mile of town. He thought that perhaps the old man hadn't been injured after all; that

82

he'd been riding hard for town to get help. Thinking like this Bond almost didn't see the head-hung silhouette of a quiet standing horse a little way northward of him until that horse, scenting Bond's mount, lifted its head and softly nickered.

The animal was saddled and bridled but he was rider-less. Bond loosened his .45 in its holster, reined off to the right and rode directly up to that saddled beast. He was rummaging the roundabout night in all directions for the person who had obviously been riding the horse, and didn't look straight down until he stopped less than ten feet off.

Then he saw him.

Old Ezra was dead, Bond realized, before he stiffly dismounted and moved reluctantly up closer. He'd been unmercifully pistol-whipped over the head, in fact both discoloration and swelling had made him nearly unrecognizable.

But it was the old man all right, and Bond went down on one knee for a closer look. He could have used more light to see by but the important things were very clear even in that gloomy atmosphere.

He stood up after a while, went back and examined Ezra's horse, got down in a low crouch to read the sign, failed because of the darkness, and finally lifted the considerable dead weight and heaved it belly down across the saddle, tied the ankles on one side, the arms on the opposite side, got back atop his own animal and resumed his way on into Jefferson.

He took the old man to a little locked shed out behind the doctor's residence, laid him out there on a table used for just this purpose, locked the door behind himself and led his horse on over to the liverybarn where a puffy-eyed and yawning nighthawk took it.

"Busy cussed night," grumbled the nighthawk. "Busiest in weeks."

"Yeah," Walt Bond said absently, and walked on down to his office to await Jubal Braden's arrival in town. For this little intervening period of time he wanted to be left alone. He'd seen his share of dead men in his time, but he'd never seen one clubbed to death before and it left him unsettled and badly shaken. He made some coffee in his office and sipped it scalding hot and black, but even that didn't work; the mood of depression was too deep.

11

JUBAL'S REACTION TO IDENTIFYING HIS FATHER'S BODY wasn't quite as Walt Bond expected. But as he thought afterwards when the pair of them sat in deep silence in his office with dawn breaking rosily around them, he wasn't exactly sure *what* he'd expected.

Jubal's jaw muscles had rippled as he'd gazed upon the old man but as far as Walt Bond could determine, that was Jubal's only show of emotion. And there in the office when Walt pressed a cup of his hot coffee upon the younger man, Jubal accepted the cup automatically and sat on as still as stone and as expressionless.

Bond said: "That accounts for Mike Leary—why he wasn't on the ranch. It also accounts for Miles lookin' so fresh for a feller who was supposed to have just got up when we knocked on the door out there."

Jubal sipped coffee, lowered the cup and continued his blinkless staring over at the opposite wall where a square of softly brightening new day light showed.

Walt said: "But that one we heard riding towards

84

town as we rode out there: I'd like to know who that was an' what he was up to."

"I'll tell you," said Jubal, his voice absolutely without inflexion. "That was Cullen. It had to be. How else would Miles and Leary know enough to be waiting out there when the old man rode up? It was Cullen; he knew the net was closing and he rode out to warn the others. When we passed him my father was already dead. Cullen was riding hard to get back to town before anyone found the old man."

"If that's so," said the constable, "then it had to be Mike Leary who led your paw's horse out there where I found him."

Jubal stirred on the chair, put aside the coffee cup and stood up. "It's daylight," he murmured. "Where does Cullen live?"

Walt also arose. "He won't be at home, he'll be at the barn. He's been showin' up down there to supervise things in the morning ever since I've known him. I'll go with you."

"No," said Jubal in that same corn husk-dry voice. "You've been up all night. You head on home."

Walt Bond's expression turned flintily obdurate. "I reckon not," he drawled, and walked on over to open the door.

They left the office almost side by side but they didn't initially get very far. Bond's daughter came walking swiftly down towards them with a shawl around her shoulders and an expression of anxiety up around her lovely eyes. She scarcely saw Jubal at all.

"Father where have you been? It's morning and you haven't been home all—"

"Honey," Bond broke in to say. "You go on back home now. I'll be along as soon I can. There's been a murder."

85

Mary Bond's violet eyes lifted to Jubal's gray, blanked-over face, lingered there uncertainly then dropped back to her father again. Walt put forth a hand to rest it lightly upon her shoulder.

"You go on home now, honey. I'll be along."

Jubal sighted a rangy figure of a man striding along up the northward plankwalk. As he watched, this lanky figure turned and swung on down into the liverybarn. It was Wilford Cullen and Jubal moved off stepping around Mary Bond. She looked swiftly upwards into Jubal's face and when he'd moved past she caught at her father, who was also heading northward, to say, "Who was it?"

"His father, honey. They beat him to death with their pistols. Now you do as I said—go on home and stay indoors. I'll be along directly."

Bond's shorter legs had to pump twice as hard to overtake big Jubal's relentless onward pacing, but the two of them were side by side again when they swung into the liverybarn.

Cullen was standing with his back to them, with his hat pushed carelessly to the back of his head, talking to his nighthawk. He didn't hear their approach until the night man, seeing Jubal's face and eyes, stepped suddenly sideways, turned and walked hastily away from there. Then Cullen turned.

Jubal didn't stop moving. His legs did; he was standing two feet off when he swung. Cullen's look of astonishment crumpled as that sledging big fist buried itself to the wrist in his soft parts. He choked, bent far over and staggered backwards, both arms locked across his middle. Jubal had the striking power of a kicking mule.

Walt Bond ripped out an oath. He hadn't expected

86

such a sudden, savage attack. He'd expected trouble all right, that's why he'd come along, but he'd been convinced there would be some preliminary discussion.

Walt was learning things about big, taciturn Jubal Braden.

He sprang ahead to get between those two larger men. He elbowed Cullen farther away and faced Jubal head on. "Don't try that again," he said, but Jubal was advancing upon Cullen now. He didn't say a word; he scarcely even glanced at Walt Bond.

The constable sprang sideways to block Jubal's inexorable, slow advance. He dropped his right hand at the same time he threw a stiff-armed left to halt Jubal. He might as well have tried to halt a falling tree with that hand. Jubal twisted past on his way around where Will Cullen was gagging.

Bond drew his .45 and took two rearward and sidewards steps to intercept Jubal again. This time he pushed his six-gun into Jubal's middle. "One more step," he said menacingly. "One more step and I'll stop you for good."

Jubal dropped his glance briefly to that gun barrel buried in his middle. He reached out with a hand to brush the thing aside. Bond cocked the gun. That sharp, deadly little sound worked its magic upon Jubal. His moving hand halted in mid-air. He raised his dry-dulled eyes to Bond's face and stood there, finally stopped.

"Back up," ordered the constable, giving his gun barrel a vicious stab deeper into Jubal's middle. "I said back up!"

Jubal didn't back up but neither did he take another onward step and Walt Bond had to be satisfied with this. He eased back on his gun hand, half twisted to see Cullen, who was straightening up with a twisted grimace across his ugly countenance, and Bond took a big step to get over on Cullen's right. With his free hand he lifted out Cullen's six-gun, poked it down the front waistband of his trousers and said, gesturing with his cocked gun, "Jubal; if you force me to, I'll do it. He's unarmed now so don't draw on him either."

Jubal didn't take his eyes off Wilford Cullen. He was again ignoring Walt Bond completely. In that lethal and inflexionless voice he said to Cullen: "Who was with you?"

Cullen's wet eyes were milky from diminishing pain. "With me—where?" he whispered. "Walt; what's the matter with him; he gone crazy or something?"

But right now Walt Bond was a poor man to turn to for sympathy or dialectic. "Answer his question!" he growled at Cullen. "Who was with you when his paw got pistol-whipped to death?"

"His paw . . . pistol-whipped to death? Gawd a'mighty, Walt, I don't know what you fellers are talkin' about."

Cullen gradually got his breath back, and with it he also got a healthy dose of fear. It was this gnawing terror in the face of Jubal's vividly obvious intentions towards him that made Will Cullen a convincing liar.

"I ain't seen his paw since yesterday when he was—"

"You are a damned liar," said Jubal, and balled up his huge fists. "You rode out to Jack Miles's place last night to warn him my paw and I knew who'd murdered my brother."

"Honest, Mister Braden, I didn't ride—"

"I'm goin' to break your neck, Cullen, with my bare hands, if you tell one more lie, Bond's six-gun notwithstanding. We *know* you went out there; we passed you as you were ridin' back to town. Now, for

88

the last time: Who was out there with you; who helped you kill my father?"

Cullen turned his gray face towards the constable. There was no help in that direction. He swung back towards Jubal and he still had both hands across his queasy middle. He jockeyed for a position of neutrality in this obvious showdown the way some men invariably do while seeking to gain time. He said, "It's true I rode out to Jack's place last night, but your paw wasn't out there."

"Was Mike Leary there?" asked Bond.

"He'd just ridden off, Jack said."

"Alone?"

Cullen raised his eyebrows. "I don't know, Walt. Jack didn't say and it wasn't important so I didn't ask, an' that's the gospel truth so help me Hannah."

Bond eased off the hammer of his gun, dropped the weapon into its holster and gazed straight over at Jubal. Bond seemed of half a mind to believe Cullen but it was impossible to tell what Jubal was thinking; his face was still totally without definable expression.

"Why did you ride out there?" asked Jubal in his dead-dry voice.

"Well," answered Cullen at once, mixing truth and prevarication in equal parts to make the thing sound believable. "Like you said—to warn Jack your pappy was goin' to make trouble for him."

"How were you so sure of that, Cullen?"

"Hell, Mister Braden, it was plumb obvious."

"I reckon it was, Cullen. Why did you lie to us about the color of the horses Leary and Sutton and Miles rode?"

"Well, I didn't know you fellers at all and they were friends of mine, Mister Braden. You'd be loyal to your friends too, wouldn't you?"

89

Jubal turned with withering scorn moving his eyes. "Do you believe any of this?" he asked Bond. The constable neither spoke nor moved his head. His brows drew inward and downward. He was positive of only one thing now: If he turned his back for a second Jubal Braden would shoot Will Cullen down in cold blood.

Bond said: "Walk out of here, Will. Head for my jailhouse."

Cullen didn't protest, in fact he seemed enormously relieved as he went wide around big Jubal towards the yonder plankwalk, his little shrewd eyes beginning to reassume their normal cunning, sly look. He turned once, just past the roadside door, and threw an eloquent stare back down where that timorous hostler was making himself as inconspicuous as possible. Jubal saw that look. So did Walt Bond. The constable gave Cullen a little rough shove and herded him southward down the plankwalk.

Jubal walked with them only as far as the first little intervening passageway between two buildings, then stepped through down there and hastened around to the back alley. There, he swung to his left, paced on up to the liverybarn's rear opening, and waited.

It wasn't a very long wait. When he heard the horse coming he stepped out, drew his gun and lifted it level with the hostler's face. "Get down off that horse," he commanded. The night man tumbled down out of the saddle turning white to the hairline.

Jubal put up his gun. The hostler was a small, wispy man without any chin and with a coarse, weak mouth.

"Where did you think you were going?" Jubal asked.

The hostler swallowed with great difficulty. He plainly didn't want to answer, yet he also just as plainly was mortally afraid not to. Ultimately he whispered:

90

"To the Miles place."

"Why?"

"To tell Jack what happened in here."

"You've been a go-between before, have you?"

"Yes, Sir. But that's all I've been, I swear to you?"

"Were you here all last night?"

"Yes, Sir."

"What time did Cullen get back to town from the Miles ranch?"

"Well; I can't rightly say. I didn't see no clock. But I'd say it was around one or one-thirty this mornin'.''

"Was his horse ridden-down?"

"Yes, Sir. It'd been rid right hard. And Will—well . . .''

"Go on. What about Will?"

"He'll shoot me for this, Mister Braden."

"He'll never shoot anyone again. Speak up, man."

"He was—scairt-lookin', and . . .''

"Go on!"

". . . An' there was blood on his shirt."

Jubal stood there considering the much smaller man for a long time. Eventually he softly said, "You've got one hour to get out of the country. After that, I'll kill you on sight."

The hostler whipped around, fumbled for the dragging reins beside him, hurled them around the horse's neck and sprang into the saddle with the agility of a small monkey. He changed course, dug in his heels and went racing southward down the alleyway instead of the original northeastward course he'd started out to take.

Jubal turned slowly to watch his progress down through town, then out onto the big prairie beyond. The hostler never once slackened off; the last Jubal saw of him both heels were rising and falling in a constant drumroll upon his speeding animal's ribs.

91

Jubal walked on down to Walt Bond's unfinished jailhouse where three men were working out the back to finish a rear wall, stepped in through the unfinished woodwork and went right on through into Bond's office. There, Wilford Cullen was seated, his face beginning to show healthy color again, and Walt Bond was scowlingly unsnarling the chains which held a set of leg-cuffs, commonly referred to in the West as "Oregon boots."

Bond glanced up. "Cells aren't finished yet," he explained. Then he said, "I didn't reckon to have any serious criminals for a while yet."

Jubal strode over and halted directly in front of seated Wilford Cullen. "It didn't work," he exclaimed. "I caught him ridin' out the back way up at the barn. He isn't going to ride out and tell Miles what's happened here, Cullen. I gave him one hour to be out of the country and at the rate he was ridin' when he left town, I think he might just make it."

Cullen sunk low in his chair, licked his lips and threw his desperate glance over where Walt Bond finally got the leg-irons untangled. He didn't say a word; obviously Cullen had no faith at all in Walt Bond's ability to intervene again if Jubal lashed out, and Cullen wasn't going to do or say a thing which might set Jubal off again.

12

AMOS REDMOND WALKED INTO BOND'S OFFICE WITH his battered face screwed down against sun glare. He saw Wilford Cullen sitting over there with leg-irons on and halted to gravely consider this.

Jubal eyed Redmond briefly then turned as though to depart from the building. Redmond said, still gazing over at Cullen, "Stay a minute, Mister Braden. This might interest you."

Jubal stopped and turned as Walt Bond came forth from a little closet where he kept his manacles and ammunition. Bond looked across at Redmond. "What's on your mind?" he asked.

"Well," answered the saloonman, nodding towards Cullen, "him, for one thing."

Bond perked up. He walked over to his desk and halted there as Redmond finally took his eyes off Cullen and passed a bundled up roll of soiled cloth across to him. Bond said: "What's this?"

Redmond swung his gaze on over to Jubal. "I live next door to Cullen," he explained. "Last night after I closed the saloon around one-thirty and went home, I saw Will come in. He stayed in his house only a few minutes then went out back where he's got a little buggy shed and he buried that there shirt Walt's holding. I watched. This morning when I got up I was still wondering, so I went over, dug the thing up—saw that blood on it—and brought it along with me to Walt's office."

Bond was holding the shirt up by the arms. The right sleeve was darkly sticky and beginning to stiffen. Bond's face was ironlike as he slowly turned towards his prisoner. "Now tell me you cut yourself shavin'," he growled.

Cullen was white. His small eyes darted about the room. Jubal, who had heard of this bloody garment from Cullen's nighthawk, stood there watching the liveryman without any expression showing at all.

Redmond said, "Walt; I thought maybe a horse

93

might've bled-out at his barn. But this mornin' I got to wondering why, if that's all it was, he snuck out there in the middle of the night and buried the shirt."

"No, it's not horse blood," said Jubal. "It's human blood, isn't it, Cullen?"

The prisoner blanched as Jubal drew upright out of a slouch as though to lunge ahead. He swung desperately appealing eyes to Constable Bond, but as before, he met with no expression of sympathy; Bond's face was closed hard against him.

"Cullen," said Jubal very softly, "I want the whole story and I want it right now."

Jubal's words fell like steel balls into that hot, still atmosphere. Cullen shrank into himself. His big nose, normally red, was gray now, and his small, swift eyes had that trapped look animals sometimes show to a hunter.

"They killed him last night. Mike and Jack. They caught him skulkin' around out there and pistol-whipped him over the head. I rode in just as they were finishin' him off. I was scairt. I whirled my horse and rode off as fast as I could back for town. Walt; you gotta believe me. That's how it happened exactly."

Jubal stepped over to Bond's desk where the constable had placed Cullen's six-gun, picked up the weapon, turned it over and examined the exposed ejector spring. He stood a long time looking downward at that gun, then, without saying a word he passed the six-gun to Walter Bond.

Redmond stepped over beside the constable to look closely at the weapon also, and it was Redmond who finally broke the stillness. "Dried blood and kinky gray hair," he said. "I suppose you loaned Mike or Jack your gun to hit Braden with, Cullen, damn your lousy soul."

Walter Bond put the gun gently back upon his table. He didn't look at Cullen now, he turned instead to closely keep an eye upon Jubal, who went over to the door and leaned there. At last emotion showed on Ezra's surviving son's face. Jubal looked ill.

Amos Redmond ran a hand through his hair and walked across where the tepid coffee was, poured himself a full cup, kept his back to Cullen while he drank the cup dry, turned back and finally looked at big Jubal. He didn't say anything.

Walt Bond opened a ledger book, briefly scrawled in it, closed the book and faced around. "I'm charging you with murder," he said thinly to Cullen. "And now I'm going to walk out to the roadway and go fetch my horse. Amos; you come along with me."

Cullen stiffened in his chair. He waited until Bond and Redmond were at the door then he broke out into nasal pleadings. "Walt; you can't do this! Don't leave me in here with Braden! Listen, Walt, we've known each other a long time—we come here in the same wagon train. You've got to give me protection; that's part of your—"

"Protection?" said Bond coldly. "Will; that's your gun on the table, and it's loaded. You don't need any more protection than that. As for Braden . . ." Bond lifted his thick shoulders and let them drop. "I haven't heard him make any threats against you in here." Bond reached for the door latch. All through this Jubal hadn't moved nor taken his eyes off Wilford Cullen.

Now Cullen heaved himself wildly upright and balanced upon his leg-ironed feet. His hands were not manacled which must have suddenly struck him as a deliberate oversight, because he cried out in a cracking

95

voice for Bond to remain, not to walk out with Redmond leaving him back there with Jubal.

But Walt opened the door and stepped on through where morning sunlight struck pitilessly out in the wide roadway, sending back a steadily bouncing light that made men pinch their eyes nearly closed.

Cullen made a last wild plea. "Walt; I'll tell you exactly what happened out there last night. The gospel truth on my word of honor. Only for gawd's sake don't leave me like this!"

Bond turned. "On your word of honor," he growled. "You never had a word of honor, Will, and you damned well know it. Everyone in town who knows you at all, knows what a louse you are."

"Listen, Walt, that old devil was goin' out there. I knew he was because I know his kind. I seen hundreds like him durin' the war. So I lit out to warn Jack; to tell him to keep a sharp watch. We split up. Jack took the out-back places behind the barn. Mike stayed over near the main house. I hid up in the hayloft. When the old devil came, he heard my horse inside and walked in. I threw down on him. We took him out in the yard. I don't know what Jack figured to do with him, but whatever it was, that old cuss let out a bellow and charged him. He dang near strangled Jack. Mike an' I jumped him from behind. We hit him over the head until he let go of Jack an' fell down."

"Yeah," said Bond icily. "Finish it, Will."

"Jack said to kill him. Mike stepped across the old man's body there in the dust and hit him three times over the head as hard as he could hit. The old man was dead. Jack sent Mike back towards town with the old devil tied across his saddle. He didn't want him found anywhere near the ranch. I left. I rode like hell to get

96

back to town before anyone knowed I was gone. I didn't know anythin' about that blood on my shirt. It was dark last night; anyway, I was shaken up pretty bad. My nighthawk said somethin' about it when I dismounted near a lantern. I run on home and buried the shirt like Amos said."

"That's all?" Walt asked.

"That's everything, Walt, from the time I rode into Jack's yard until I got back to town again. That's exactly how it happened, I swear it."

Jubal turned, sickened, and shouldered out past Bond and Redmond to get where there was no vision of Cullen's ugly, contorted face, and where there was good air to breathe.

Bond stepped back inside, crossed to a heavy steel ring bolted to the wall, jerked his head at Cullen and when the wilted, wringing wet liveryman moved over in a series of little hops and jumps, Bond padlocked his leg-irons to the steel ring, checked his handiwork to be certain Cullen couldn't possibly get free, then he rejoined Amos Redmond and Jubal out on the hot plankwalk, closed the office door and dropped his hand to his side at the same time letting off a long, ragged exhaled breath.

He finally said to Jubal: "You want to stay; maybe see the doc before they embalm your father, or ride with me?"

Jubal faced around, pushed sweat off his gray cheeks and forehead with a shirtsleeve, and jutted his chin in the direction of the liverybarn. "I'll ride with you," he said.

Amos Redmond also said he'd ride with Walt, but Bond declined his offer, stating that until he returned Amos could serve him better if he'd remain behind in

97

town and look in on the prisoner from time to time. Redmond didn't argue but he didn't look pleased with his role either. He had no idea at the time what a spot Walt had put him in. Neither, for that matter, did Constable Bond or Jubal.

They got their horses at the untended liverybarn, saddled up in total silence, mounted and rode on out into the sun-blasted roadway, turned left and walked along until they were clear of the traffic and the dust of Jefferson.

They bore northeastward in a steady long lope, eventually, and hauled back down to a fast walk when the first sheen of sweat appeared upon their animals. They were within a mile of the Miles ranch by then, and Walt, who had been the leader, pointed earthward.

"Cullen finally told the truth. There are only two sets of tracks. One belonged to your father's horse, the other one belonged to Leary's animal."

Jubal, who had also been studying this sign, nodded. He didn't speak. Hadn't spoken in fact since before they'd left town.

Jack Miles's buildings ultimately appeared up off the eastward plain. There was a dull sheen of dust hanging over the yonder yard.

Constable Bond slowed his horse and peered ahead for sign of men or movement. There was none. He twisted up his mouth in a bitter expression but he didn't say what he now was thinking. That dust had been scuffed to life by horsemen; he didn't believe they were going to find either Miles or Leary at the ranch.

He was correct.

They passed into the yard feeling that emptiness ranchyard's oftentime have when there's not a soul on the place. They tied up at the barn and slow-paced their way over to the bunkhouse, entered and surveyed the mussed up little room. There was nothing there they hadn't previously seen so they walked on across to Miles's house and Walt Bond threw a thick shoulder against the barred door. It finally took the combined heft of the pair of them to break that stubborn latch.

Miles's home was cool, dingy, and sparsely furnished. It was typical of a bachelor cowman's establishment. They went through the rooms without actually hoping for anything until Jubal paused beside a hastily slammed drawer which was partially open, drew the drawer open wider and bent to pick something up. Walt turned and watched. Jubal held up a long-barrelled old rebored Dragoon revolver.

"My father's," he said, and pushed the big pistol into his belt. "I've seen enough. Let's go."

"Where?" asked Bond. "They could be out on the range."

"Maybe they are," Jubal assented, "but up to now they only know we suspect. They don't know that we have all the proof we need. So—they'll head for town sometime today."

Bond thought a moment on this then followed Jubal back out into the yard and across to their horses. They rode out of the yard the same southwestward way they'd ridden in, only now Jubal opened up a little.

"Constable; I'm beholden for all you've done in this."

"It's my job, Jubal."

"Well . . . what comes next is *my* job. I'd appreciate it if you'd manage to be somewhere else for a while when they ride into Jefferson."

Walt got that same obdurate expression again. "Sorry," he quietly exclaimed. "Not a chance of that. Why d'you think I've been stickin' to you like a cockleburr? So's you won't do anything you'll spend the next fifty years regrettin'."

"Constable, I won't regret anything I do to those men."

"Not even shooting them down in cold blood or from behind?"

"Not even that, Constable. I'm going to kill them any way that I can, an' if you happen to jump in between again like you did with Cullen . . . ." Jubal turned directly towards Walt Bond. "Then I'll kill you too."

Bond rode along strongly silent until they had Jefferson in sight again. Then he said, "Jubal; I'm a little bit afraid of what the future holds for both of us. I never wanted to shoot a man less than I do you, but make no mistakes, boy. Make no mistakes at all about my ability to do it if you force me to."

13

THE MINUTE THEY HIT TOWN THEY BOTH KNEW something was wrong. People, for instance, were gathered in little groups along the plankwalk quietly talking. As Bond and Jubal Braden rode down into town men turned to look outward into the dazzling roadway, to watch their progress towards the uncompleted jailhouse.

Walt swung down over there and still with one hand upon his saddlehorn turned to make a slow survey of the roadway. That was when a female hand opened the jailhouse door behind him and his daughter walked out. Her face was pink from exertion and her eyes were dark with anxiety. She stood a moment gazing at big Jubal and her father, then she said, "In here."

Walt crossed over in large strides. He had a premonition. Jubal was right behind him with the same bad feeling. Mary stepped back until they were inside, then gently closed the door.

"It's Amos," Mary whispered to her father, nodding over where two men stood bent over a prone man upon a little narrow iron cot.

Jubal, seeing only those two bent over strangers in the office with Amos Redmond, swung on the girl. "Where's Cullen?" he sharply demanded.

"Gone," said Mary Bond.

Walt spun around. "Gone?"

"Yes. About fifteen minutes after you two rode out Jack Miles and Mike Leary rode into town. Amos was the only one who knew what was going on. If others had known perhaps Amos wouldn't be lying there now. Miles and Leary heard that you two had arrested Wilford Cullen. They came down here. Amos was sitting in here when they burst in. He tried to stop them; he rushed them. Leary struck him over the head, hard. He's been unconscious for almost an hour now. They released Cullen and the three of them ran for their horses and fled out of town southward towards the mountains."

Walt Bond ground out a rasping oath and went across where those two men were standing above the unconscious man. As the constable came up one of those men turned. He was tall and youthful with a long, grave face and thick eyeglasses. This one said, "Walt; it's a pretty serious wound. Leary must've struck him with everything he had."

Bond shouldered in for a closer look. Jubal also walked over. Amos Redmond had a bloody, matted big welt down one side of his head. He was feebly breathing and from time to time his eyelids faintly fluttered.

101

Jubal said to that long-faced young man. "Are you the doctor?" The young man nodded. "What are his chances?"

"Without trying to be reassuring I'd say they were fair. Amos Redmond's got a thick skull. I've tended him before. Any other man would be dead from that blow. But he'll be several weeks getting over this beating. It was needlessly savage."

Mary Bond went to a chair and sank down. When her father passed over to that little closet and disappeared briefly inside she watched for him to reemerge, and when he did, holding a stubby .30-.30 and two boxes of bullets, she said, "I watched; they went straight towards the foothills. But there are the three of them and you'll need—"

"Only me," stated Jubal quietly. "I know those southward hills better than anyone hereabouts."

Mary lifted her eyes to Jubal. She seemed to regard him both accusingly and pityingly. "Please be careful, both of you," she murmured. "Don't worry about Amos, Dad; I'll stay here until you get back."

Walt went over, handed Jubal one of the boxes of carbine shells, jerked his head and started across for the roadside doorway. Mary got up and swiftly went over where her father and big Jubal were heading out. She said to Jubal: "He hasn't had any sleep in twenty-four hours. Please he's not a young man any more . . ."

"I'll watch out for him," murmured Jubal, and held this beautiful girl's glance for a second longer. "He'll come back, ma'am, don't worry about that."

She put up a hand to squeeze Jubal's arm, then turned to smile out at her father who was beside his horse at the hitchrack, his face set in an unrelenting and iron like expression. "Good hunting, Dad," she called. Walt didn't look up right away. When he did he simply nodded at her, turned and swung up over leather and sat there gazing through narrowed eyes towards the far-away southward rims while he waited for Jubal, pointing earthward, said, "Good, fresh tracks. There's dust all the way to the foothills. We can make a little time."

After that they loped.

The sun was still hot although as the afternoon advanced it lost some of that brassy hue and turned softer shades of pink and red.

Jubal unthinkingly took the lead at what they were now about, for as he'd said, he knew those onward mountains. Bond had nothing to say until they were close enough to make out the little crooked hunters' trail winding upwards along a naked sidehill.

"They've got about a two hour lead."

Jubal was unimpressed. "It won't help them unless they know the hills. Strangers up in there can lose two hours without even trying. We'll find them."

"Unless they split up," muttered the grim-faced lawman, and rode steadily along studying the yonder slopes for a while before he also said, "Amos is a friend of mine. He never carried a gun."

Jubal turned to consider Bond's face. It occurred to him that now, at long last, Walter Bond was as aroused to merciless, cold and calculating wrath towards those three killers as he also was. As they went along side by side Jubal detachedly wondered what Bond's reaction would be when the five of them met back in the lawless mountains somewhere with no one to witness what would happen. He thought he knew; thought he understood the kind of a man Walter Bond was. And yet he had his small doubts too; as a lawman, Bond had his obligations to the justice he served.

Jubal eventually put aside these speculations. He would find out about Bond soon enough. Meanwhile, he had a trail to follow and this wasn't going to be easy after they crossed the top-out, because from up there that failing sun wouldn't shine down the far side, he wouldn't be able to accurately track Miles, Leary and Cullen, and if those three kept on riding they just might put a lot of miles between their pursuers and themselves before fresh daylight returned.

This dilemma held most of Jubal's attention as they came into the first little rising foothills that presaged the still higher country to come. They left the big prairie behind, starting steadily upwards along the old trail. The tracks of three ridden, shod horses lay conveniently ahead of them on up the path.

Once Constable Bond said: "The fools; any idiot would know better than to keep to a trail like this."

"They had no other choice," Jubal explained. "Whether they knew it or not this is the only through-trail between your prairie back there and my high desert country on ahead."

Bond said no more. He evidently wasn't too familiar with the country they were passing over. When they eventually reached the saddle and halted to briefly rest their mounts, Walt twisted for a rearward look. The sun was beginning to lose even its dull, afternoon lustre now. Out upon the huge prairie there lay a soft, benighted pre-evening glow. Down the southward side of the mountains were patches of shade which, even as they watched, deepened into dusky shadows.

Jubal was impatient. He pushed on watching the tracks. They were part way down the hillside towards a

104

gloomy forested pocket where the trail dipped low then rose up on the pocket's far side, before they lost the tracks for the first time because of gloom. Jubal rode on to the next place where fading light lay, picked up the tracks and made his beast move along a little faster. Bond kneed his animal along to keep up, but his expression was turning gloomy now. Clearly, he didn't think they were going to speedily overtake those three killers after all.

But Jubal, who had lived in these mountains, knew the ways of reading sign even where the trail faded out entirely; where the forested slopes piled up around them cutting off their forward sight. An observant man didn't have to always rely upon his eyes. For example, the forest was ordinarily a noisy place where scurrying small creatures bustled about their normal activities and where birds sang and scolded and endlessly argued with one another. When a man rode through a thoroughly hushed forest he could be certain that something of which all forest-creatures stood in mortal dread, had just passed along ahead of him. Usually, this could be a mountain lion, a bear—or men. A knowledgeable horseman could track down his prey simply by keeping well within that perimeter of total silence; following it to where some knoll or peak or spiny wind-scourged ridge permitted him to stand entirely still watching for movement.

In a large forest, as upon a big plain, movement stood out at once to anyone watching for it. If dusk limited the visibility, then there was another way: Evening was the one time of day when noise carried farthest. A listener could hear a horseshoe strike upon stone for a mile or better; could discern the abrasive rub of squeaking leather or the swish of a horseman passing through underbrush. There were many varied ways for pursuers to detect the presence of their enemies in a chase such as this, providing they knew the ways of doing it, and Jubal did.

He stopped once where the trail levelled off, sat for a long time without moving even an eyelid, then he led off again without saying a word. Constable Bond, sustained by his bitter thoughts, trailed along bleakly silent.

They crossed forth and back where a crooked little whitewater creek tumbled brawlingly down towards the high desert country dimly discernible ahead. This was Braden Creek; it ran past out behind the Braden ranch buildings.

They dipped far down into a cool shallow canyon and climbed back out again, always keeping to the ageless Indian trail, and as they persevered each rode with his secret thoughts and his tireless wish for harsh vengeance.

The sun left them entirely, at last, its departure laying a long moment of stillness over the upland, forested world they rode through. By then they had the high desert well in view and rearward the peaks formed a timeless backdrop. They were not far from the Braden homeplace; each onward step of their horses jarred Jubal to a difficult acceptance that neither his father nor his brother would ever again sing out to him as he rode down into the ranch yard. At first he didn't want to see the log house, the barn, the faggot-fenced garden patch, but just after the glow of starshine with their animals beginning to lag, beginning to show the tiredness their gruelling pace had exacted from them, he caught sight of the buildings down there in their little hidden cove where hillside shoulders richly turned and bunched up to protect the Braden place, and it didn't pain him as much as he'd anticipated. In fact he felt relieved to be home again.

But Walt Bond's low growl wrenched him away from nostalgia and the confusion of his other emotions in a second. Bond said, "Westerly there—I saw a little light. Who'd be down at those buildings; 'you know?"

Jubal swung his glance to westward. That was where the horses usually grazed. He watched closely but saw no light. "No one'd be at those buildings," he muttered. "That's the Braden ranch—my home. There's no one there."

"Someone's there all right," mumbled the lawman. "That was a match or a candle, or something like that, and it was off to the west a ways."

Jubal moved on as far as the last little rise before the trail dropped straight down towards the buildings, and there he reined up turning thoughtful. Those three stud colts John was to have altered would be over westerly, with the other horses and probably some of their cattle too, because that was where a tributary of Braden Creek made a pool with tender grass around it.

Riders coming hastily down out of the hills with daylight around them, if they needed fresh horses, would have spied that pool and the band of horses around it; would in all probability have made for that place to get replacements for their wearying mounts.

The prospect of finding the men they sought without additional pursuit quickened his awareness, lifted his tired spirits. He jerked his head at Bond and left the trail heading off westerly through the murky forest. For half a mile he rode along then stopped near a madrone thicket, tied his horse and beckoned for Bond to come along.

They slipped down to the last diminishing lift of land, each with his carbine, each moving with all the careful stealth they were capable of.

Beyond the last tier of pines the high desert lay eerily starlighted, empty and ancient with its soft shadings of ghostly paleness. Several huge old ragged cottonwoods and poplars grew down by the pool and where the tributary creek ran into this place it tumbled over smooth-worn rock making a soft rustling sound. It was this steady noise which kept any sound of their coming from the horses down there at the poolside but obviously something else had captured their attention for the horses were standing stiffly, their heads facing back around easterly. They seemed to be on the verge of bolting.

Jubal dropped to one knee, his right hand supporting his Winchester, and carefully keened the night. He saw no light and in fact Constable Bond never saw it again either, but both of them could clearly tell that something had those horses worried.

"Making a surround," suggested the lawman. "Probably one's comin' at 'em from each side with lariats."

Jubal said nothing but he doubted that this was so. For one thing the horses were all watching the same easterly direction. For another thing they'd encountered no one up in the forest fringe.

He eventually sighted a faint blur of movement coming in from the east. Whoever this man was he was wisely keeping the cottonwoods between himself and the suspicious horses. When that man finally got close to a tree and straightened up, Jubal recognized him: Will Cullen!

14

WALTER BOND LET HIS BREATH OUT IN A LONG, LOW
sigh. He said nothing but he'd obviously also
recognized the lanky Kentuckian. The only time Walt
moved was when Jubal slowly lifted his carbine,
snugged it back with a bead drawn on the escaped
prisoner then Bond put up an arm, took firm hold of
Jubal's rifle barrel and forced it gradually downward.
He shook his head.

"He gets one chance to quit," Bond whispered,
"before we kill him."

Jubal lowered the gun and watched Cullen for a
minute. The liveryman was good at stalking; he angled
absolutely without sound until he was slightly above
and behind those uneasy horses. If he was as good with
the lariat he was carrying as he was at this stalking, he
would probably catch a horse. The trouble was, as Jubal
saw it, that in the poor light of evening Cullen,
experienced horseman that he was, could not make out
which horses were broken to saddle and which, like
those big stud colts, were as wild as a March hare. He
thought, as he watched, that the killer was making his
selection now.

Cullen stood beside a rough-barked tall poplar with
his loop built, with his coiled loose rope and its turk's-
head end, firmly in each hand. He was ready to make
his cast but he kept studying those horses at poolside. A
powerful black was closest to him. Jubal knew that
horse; it was the largest of the three stud colts, was
nearly four years old and had never in its life had a rope
on it. If Cullen roped that one he'd never in God's green
world be able to hold it. Cullen weighed about one

hundred and sixty pounds, the black colt weighed at least twelve hundred pounds.

But Wilford Cullen, the lifelong horseman, was no fool. He carefully bent and carefully made the turk's-head end of the rope fast to the trunk of the poplar. Whatever the big black did now, one thing he *wouldn't* do was get clean away.

Bond started to move, to struggle back up to his feet with his .30-.30 held crossways to his body. Jubal checked him with an out-flung arm. He whispered: "Watch. Leave him an' just watch. He thinks he's picking out the stoutest of our horses. Actually, he's pickin' the meanest, wildest of our unbroke stud colts. That horse's never had a rope on him. Cullen couldn't get a saddle on him even if he can rope him."

Bond knelt back down but from time to time he glanced eastward over towards the dark and gloomy distant ranch buildings.

Cullen was ready. He paused one more moment then stepped out, made his one head-encircling backhand cast before all the horses caught sight of that movement and sprang to life, and his cast was true. The rope sang high up and far out. It settled expertly around the big black colt's neck. The colt gave a tremendous jump the second that rope touched him. He hit the end of it with the other horses scattering wildly in every direction. The rope sang taut, the colt went end over end, and a great gobbet of dust jerked to life where he hit the ground.

Cullen started down the rope. He still hadn't figured out that he had a wild one on the end of his lariat. Most ranch bred saddle animals reacted like this when roped without warning; the tamest old pelter in a corral full of broken horses would fight a rope when it struck him unexpectedly. Cullen kept going down the rope hand

110

over hand, his face intent and soft-lighted, his body jerking with the wild threshings coming up the rope to him. Jubal and Walt Bond were tense; were living this moment right along with Will Cullen.

The stud-colt sprang up, set his legs wide and stood out there at the constricting end of the lariat rolling his eyes and quivering all over. Cullen started a crooning conversation as he moved on up. When he was about five feet away he halted, put his head a little to one side as though gradually wondering whether or not he'd made a bad mistake, and he became silent. Possibly it was Cullen's sweaty, rank smell, possibly it was his sudden silence and nearness, but the colt abruptly exploded, as terrified horses will. He couldn't go backwards, which would have been his choice of directions if he'd *had* a choice, and he could only rock a little from side to side, so, his only recourse was to hurl himself straight ahead, which is what he did. He gave a tremendous onward bound, rising in the air as though to jump over Wilford Cullen, but he'd lacked the adequate start for so high a jump and when he struck Cullen it was his chest, shoulders and upper legs which caught the liveryman. Cullen gave a shrill outcry. He tried to fling clear but the horse had exploded too quickly. Cullen went down to one knee. He threw both arms up in front of his face and jerked upright as the black colt flashed past.

Jubal was afterwards convinced that if Cullen hadn't sprang right back up he'd have got off with only a little wind knocked out of him, but when he jumped up as the colt ducked past, the horse let fly with his left hind foot, the hoof of which was like iron from years of running unshod on the high desert.

Jubal and Bond heard the crunching sound as that

111

powerful kick connected. They saw Cullen's arms fling wide like the limp arms of a doll. Cullen was knocked clear off his feet, sailed over towards the forest fringe, and collapsed in a broken heap.

The stud-colt had sixty feet to reach his peak speed before hitting the end of that lariat again. When he came to the end the identical thing occurred again. He was abruptly checked in headlong flight, his head went down, his hind quarters sailed high, and he turned a complete pinwheel in the air before striking the ground with sufficient force to make the earth reverberate up where Jubal and Walt were standing. But the rope broke, and although the panicked horse fought his way numbly back to his feet, he didn't try to run again, not for some time. He was knocked half unconscious by the fall.

Jubal stepped past the last line of trees with his carbine in his right hand. He covered the intervening space to Cullen's side in six or eight big strides. Walt Bond came forth from the forest also. The pair of them stood gazing at awkwardly sprawling Wilford Cullen.

"Plumb in the guts," said Bond softly. "I heard it hit him all the way up where we were watchin'."

Jubal handed Walt his Winchester, knelt and straightened the fugitive's arms and legs, then went to poolside, scooped up a hatful of water, went back and trickled it over Cullen's ashen face. There was a slow trickle of blood running from Cullen's mouth. They propped him up comfortably, disarmed him, and continued to run cold water over him until Cullen's eyelids flickered, lifted and dropped, then eventually lifted and hung partly open for the long moment Cullen focused his eyes upon the two kneeling men beside him. He tried to say something, coughed claret, spat and tried again.

112

"Roped me a damned—wild colt."

Jubal nodded. "We were watching, Cullen. That stud-colt's never been roped or handled before in his life."

". . . My luck . . . to pick a wild one."

"Where are Miles and Leary?" Walt Bond asked.

". . . Miles . . . Leary? Gone."

"Gone where?"

Cullen weakly rolled his head from side to side. "Don't know. My horse played out. They said they'd go on . . . If I could, I was to catch up."

"Which direction?" Bond asked insistently as Cullen's words began to slur, as his eyes began to turn dry and unusually dark with a milkiness.

" . . .West. Went west. Hey, Walt; remember when we first came out here?"

Bond and Jubal exchanged a glance. Jubal shrugged. Evidently that terrific kick in the middle had broken Cullen up badly inside. The trickle of crimson at the corner of his mouth was running faster now.

"Hemorrage," murmured Jubal, "No one to save him this far from town and the doctor back there."

Bond leaned closer. "Will; you hear me? Listen: What does Miles have in mind doing?"

There was no answer. The dark trickle at the edge of Cullen's lips ceased flowing. He was looking unblinkingly straight up into Jubal's face.

Bond gently shook him by the shirt front. "Will? Will? Hang on a minute."

Jubal stood up, grounded his Winchester and leaned gravely upon it. "No use," he said softly. "Cullen's dead."

Bond rocked back on his heels. "Dammit," he growled fretfully, and scowled at the dead man.

Jubal lifted big shoulders and dropped them. "He told

113

us enough. Give me a hand. We'll lug him into the barn and leave him there until we can send someone out to fetch him into Jefferson for burial."

They carried Cullen all the way over to the dark buildings, into the barn, and left him lying upon a little rick of loose hay. But as they walked back outside, from off easterly and higher up, came the bitterly complaining whimperings of a bear which had evidently heard them, had been aroused from its bed and was now shambling on down to investigate. Walt Bond whirled and whipped up his carbine. This time it was Jubal who forced the gun barrel downward.

"An old pet," he said, as that moldy old gummer she-bear came crashing out of the creekside underbrush to lift her head high, sniffing. She was, like all bears, endowed with very poor eyesight even in broad daylight, but now, in the night, she had to rely exclusively upon her nose, which she now did.

Bond lowered his carbine but he kept a wary eye upon the old mammy. "Fine thing to have for a pet," he muttered.

Jubal was briefly thoughtful, then turned back towards the barn. "Come on," he said with a minimum amount of explaining. "We can't leave Cullen in here after all. We'll lock him inside the house where she won't be able to get to him."

Bond angled around, when they returned for Cullen and were carrying him over towards the house, so that he always had one eye on that whining, swaying old she-bear over near the creekside underbrush.

After they'd put Cullen where he'd be safe from meat eating animals, Jubal went out to the smokehouse, hacked off a haunch and carried it over to the old bear. She accepted it with her usual show of bad manners,

114

turned her back on him, sat down and went to work. Walt Bond watched all this from over across the yard. When Jubal returned and the pair of them started back where their horses were, Walt said, "I'd shoot that damned varmint."

Jubal said nothing. He walked along thoughtfully until they got back to their mounts. Then he untied, stepped across leather and looked off on his left. "Westerly there's nothing but the high desert and the foothills for several days' ride, and I reckon that makes sense for Miles and Leary. Let's go."

"You know that country as well as this end of it?" Bond asked.

Jubal nodded and led out.

After a while the moon rose, its yellow, ancient light brightening the high desert to a soft butter color. They encountered little bunches of cattle here and there, bedded down and docile except where a mighty old horned bull rose up to trumpet a challenge at the riders. Jubal regarded the scarred big beast and said, "That's Jeff Davis. My paw named him when we were drivin' him up into this high country from down below where we traded some cows for him."

Bond rolled his eyes at the ton of massive animal. "Why Jeff Davis?" he inquired.

Jubal made the first smile he'd shown in some time, but it only touched his long lips. "The old man said he was a nosy old busybody; said he reminded him of old Jeff Davis, the Confederacy's president."

Bond eyed the bull soberly until they were well past. "Your paw was a Reb, is that it?"

"He was."

They had no more to say to one another until, about five miles along out upon the vast emptiness of the high

115

desert, Jubal abruptly swung over into the trees and rode along through this more difficult place.

"You figure they might be stopping along here some place?" asked Constable Bond.

Jubal shrugged. "There's a cow camp a couple miles farther along. They're bound to see the pole corrals and the signs of a camp. We called it Blueberry Camp. I have a hunch they might at least investigate it." He turned towards the lawman. "What's puzzlin' me is why they didn't stop and also try to get fresh horses back at the pool. If Cullen saw those animals out there Miles and Leary must also have seen them."

Bond rocked along running this through his mind. Eventually he said, "Maybe they *did* see those loose horses, and maybe they also figured pursuit would be close behind. It that's so, why then they wouldn't take the chance Cullen took. Of course, if Will's horse gave out on him, he had no other choice. But I also think Jack and Mike—and I know 'em both well enough to believe 'em capable of this—would be perfectly willing for us to catch Cullen an' be delayed by him so that they could put more miles under their saddles." Bond pinched his eyes nearly closed as he pursued this train of thought. He ultimately said, "Y'know, Jubal, that black stud-colt just might have done us a real service."

"How's that?"

"We didn't fire a shot and neither did Cullen. Miles and Leary would have been able to hear gunshots for five miles, up in this high desert country. They *didn't* hear any, so they might think we aren't very close behind 'em."

Jubal considered this and found it plausible. Whether the fleeing killers had actually been listening for sounds of a fight or not, he knew one thing for a fact. What

116

Bond had said about the noise traveling five miles out was perfectly true. He also reasoned that Miles and Leary couldn't be more than perhaps three or four miles ahead of them, so, if there *had* been a gunfight, whether the killers had been intentionally listening or not, they'd have heard it.

Cullen *had* delayed them too. Originally, he didn't think the fugitives had been more than two miles ahead of them. Now though, he felt certain they were close to five miles ahead.

15

THEY CAME TO BLUEBERRY CAMP WITH THE QUIET hush of full night all round them. They left their horses back in the trees again and cautiously scouted ahead until they were satisfied neither Miles nor Leary were there.

But they had *been* there, and they had rested. There was plenty of sign around; wet boot tracks over near the creek and some hastily gnawed tender grass shoots where their hungry horses had utilised that brief respite to fill out the pleats in their bellies.

Then Walt Bond came upon a puzzling thing. "Here," he called softly to Jubal. "Come take a look at these tracks."

It was difficult to make out anything because of tree shadows and the weak overhead light. Had they been on horseback they would have missed the tracks entirely. But they were on foot, so Jubal bent far over to study the sign Walt had discovered. It was the faintly damp imprint of a horse's worn shoe—pointing westerly.

Jubal went back a foot at a time until he found where

a second ridden horse joined the first one. Both those animals were retracing their former route. He straightened up to gaze at Walt and scratch his head. They had both just come from the west and neither of them had seen or heard anything.

"Swung south," suggested Bond. "If they hadn't we'd surely have bumped into them." Walt turned and stared back down the night. "But what are they up to, I'd like to know?"

Jubal was silently thoughtful for a long time while he tried to puzzle this out. That Miles and Leary had gone back westward again, retracing their earlier trail, was indisputable. But it took him a little while to figure out why and how this could be so.

"I'm guessing," he eventually said, in a slow drawl. "But if they didn't hear any sounds of a fight back there at the ranch they'd believe the pursuit, if there was any, was still a long way off, wouldn't they?"

"Yes, I reckon so," assented Bond.

"And if their horses are as done for as Cullen's was, then they'd realize they had to get fresh animals, wouldn't they?"

Bond slowly nodded without speaking. He was obviously beginning to understand how Jubal's thoughts were turning.

"But to be plenty safe they decided to go far down the southward desert, then, when they were even with the ranch, to ride straight northward again on up to the pool where they left Cullen."

"One thing," exclaimed the lawman. "How well would those two know the westward country?"

Jubal looked wry. "You've said yourself those men rode out a lot, here and there. I'm guessin' they know damned well that for two days' steady riding westerly

118

there are no more ranches where they can steal fresh horses. Within two days their animals would put them afoot from exhaustion and poor care. I think they've just come to that, Constable. I figure they're going back while they believe the trail is still safe for them, to get two fresh animals."

"We can't beat them to the ranch and they'll find Cullen. They'll know something's wrong."

Jubal turned towards his patient horse. "No. If we'd left him in the barn they'd have found him. But I doubt if they'll take the time to break in the house. They know there's nothing in any of the buildings they want, and they'll be in a hurry to get fresh animals and head on out. Come on, Constable; let's make tracks out of here."

As Bond mounted up, reined around and followed Jubal back up into the forest fringe, he said, "Maybe that consarned bear helped us without knowing it, makin' us move Cullen into the house."

Jubal kept to the trees for a mile for caution's sake, then, in order to make better time, he angled back down out onto the moonwashed big plain where they could lope for almost another two miles. After that in order to favor their horses, they rode side by side at a steady fast walk.

The hour was late when eventually they caught the first faint square blackness of the Braden barn roof. Bond was in favor of abandoning the horses and going the rest of the way afoot, but Jubal disagreed by simply riding on until they were close enough to make out all the familiar sites on ahead. Then he dismounted, drew forth his Winchester, hid his horse in the forest where it was unlikely to be found, and started on stealthily towards the northward slope up behind the ranchyard.

Walt Bond moved as quietly as he also could, but

119

Walt was wearying; he lacked almost twenty years of being as young as Jubal was, had been without food or rest for over twenty-four hours, and, as much as he deplored the murders which had brought him after Leary and Miles, he had very little of that white-hot motivation which kept Jubal functioning at peak efficiency. Even Walt's initial wrath over the pointless clubbing down of Amos Redmond had been blunted by this time because he was satisfied that Amos would survive.

What he wanted most of all now, was to get this chase over with one way or another. Secondly, he wanted to prevent Jubal from also committing murder. Not that he felt any pity for Miles or Leary, but because he knew what that kind of a conscience can do to a young man who has to live with it for the rest of his long life.

They were almost in place up near the old Indian trail when a horse nickered somewhere southward in the velvet night, bringing them both to an immediate, crouching halt.

"Could be your loose stock," mumbled Bond.

"Could be Miles and Leary, too," answered Jubal right back. "Stay here. I'm going eastward over where I can see the pool."

"In a pig's eye," growled Bond, and when Jubal started off the constable went right along behind him.

Jubal made no protest beyond briefly regarding Bond with a look of disapproval.

They passed well eastward, saw the pool, and up above them in the trees and underbrush heard an animal's careless noises. Bond whipped around bringing his carbine to bear but Jubal wagged his head, slipped back a hundred feet where Bond heard him softly speaking in a coaxing tone. Moments later Jubal returned and sank down beside his tense companion.

Bond growled: "That damned she-bear."

"Guess again; it was Cullen's horse. I unsaddled it and took off the bridle. It's lame in a hind foot and it's been badly abused. I expect that's the horse we heard nicker a while back."

"You left it loose?" demanded the constable.

"Why not?" Jubal countered, settling around to watch the open country. "If Miles and Leary find it they'll only believe Cullen abandoned it after getting a fresh horse. That's why I off-saddled it. If they saw it with a saddle on they'd know cussed well something was wrong. Cullen wouldn't ride away on a fresh horse without his outfit."

Walt Bond eased down in the underbrush with a half-groan, half-sigh. He joined Jubal in watching the pool which lay several hundred yards southward, just beyond the last tier of timber.

"No horses," he grunted. "Maybe they'll run across them farther out."

"Maybe," agreed Jubal. "Whatever they do we're bound to hear them."

Moments passed; minutes turned into long and continuing passages of flowing time. Overhead, the sky kept its enamelled blackness, the moon seemed scarcely to be moving at all and stars by the millions shone with a winking, cold, cold light. Down at the buildings, visible off on their left, to the eastward, there was a depthless stillness that had a sad and melancholic hush to it. Evidently the old she-bear had long since taken her deer haunch up creek to some secret place she knew of, to whimperingly gnaw upon, but wherever she was neither Walt Bond nor Jubal could hear her, and that

121

could mean only one thing, since bears are notoriously garrulous, always bitterly complaining and making their snuffling sounds, she had to be a long way off.

A man's quiet call sang down the night from out upon the high desert. There were no distinguishable words to that call, just the lifting, fluting sound of a man's bass voice hailing someone else out there.

"Due south," muttered Bond.

"And coming straight on towards us," complemented Jubal.

An answering cry came back leading Jubal and Walt Bond to believe the killers had split up in their search for the Braden horse herd.

The recognizable voice of Jack Miles said: "Anything, Mike?"

And Leary's quick answer floated strongly right back: "Not out here, Jack. Maybe they're up at the danged pool or maybe Will done spooked 'em out of the country catchin' his replacement."

"The pool," sang out Miles. "Meet me over at the pool."

Jubal craftily and promptly glided down another hundred feet until he was almost in among the last stand of shielding trees. Constable Bond trailed along behind him. They took their fresh position carefully and crouched there waiting.

Jack Miles appeared as a vague moving mounted silhouette well beyond rifle range southward. Jubal raised his gun, rested its barrel in the crotch of a seedling pine, and for once Walt Bond did not deter him.

But Miles didn't come on up into range. From eastward among the log buildings Mike Leary's youthful voice rose into the dark hush. "Hey, Jack;

there's a fresh grave over here. Come take a look."

Miles halted and twisted in the saddle as he called back, his voice sounding irritable. "Damn it, of course there's a grave over there. That's where they buried the one we killed the night we came up here for their cache."

Bond saw Jubal's knuckle tighten spasmodically around the carbine trigger. Walt held his breath. He thought surely Jubal would fire. He thought, too, that the range was much too great for a short-barrelled Winchester saddle gun, and he was correct.

But Jubal didn't fire. He also knew how small his chances were of reaching Miles.

Leary called out once more. "Hey, Jack; this damned house is locked."

Miles let off a string of harsh curses. "Forget the lousy cabin," he said angrily. "Come on over here by the pool. If the blamed horses are up here I can only rope one for myself. Get on over here and catch your own critter."

But Leary didn't obey. Instead, he said, with a little perplexed drag to his voice. "Jack, I'm tellin' you *the house is locked!* Use your head. When we was here with Will I entered this cabin lookin' for tinned food to pack along. *The door wasn't locked then!*"

Constable Bond groaned. Jubal gradually lowered his carbine, swung to peer off towards the ranch buildings and appeared for a long moment to be holding his breath. Then, as Miles turned, still well beyond carbine range, to ride slowly and silently over in the direction Leary had been speaking from, Jubal rapped Walt Bond sharply on the arm and jerked his head. The pair of them went stealthily slipping back the way they had come.

They reached the hunters' trail, crossed it eastward,

stepped into a lower down trampled place which still smelled of horses although none had been tethered here since that black night when John Braden had been shot down, and here they paused with an excellent in-range view of the main log ranch house.

Miles was tantalizingly slow in arriving down there. Leary was in sight, temptingly so, with his back to the hidden men, facing that locked cabin door, his carbine grounded beside him.

Miles left his horse on the south side of the cabin and took two steps around the front wall, shot a look eastward, and ripped out a wild curse as he skipped high, flung around and jumped back out of sight around the corner.

All this had evidently taken young Mike Leary quite by surprise. He spun twistingly around to shoot a quick look eastward, too, but he didn't move for almost five seconds. Not until Miles hissed at him.

"Get away from the front, Mike. *Move dammit!*"

Mike moved. He flung himself around the northward corner of the house where that fresh grave was.

"What is it?" he panted in a shrill voice. "Jack what'n hell spooked you?"

Jubal was curious about that too. So was Walt Bond. Until Miles reversed himself so quickly they both had been confident of a quick capture or a quick kill. Now, although they still could vaguely make out Leary's silhouette, Miles was entirely lost to them.

"A reflection," said Miles. "It looked like moonlight off a rifle barrel."

"Where?" demanded Leary, back-stepping until John's mounded grave halted him. "Where, Jack?"

"Yonder in those eastward trees where we left the horses that other time we was up here."

Jubal put his carbine down upon the ground. Bond also did this, but Walt went even further with his caution; he got down on both knees and bent until nothing could be seen of him through the thick-standing undergrowth.

For a full minute there was a tense, hushed silence. Miles's head, near the ground, was invisible because of the layers of nighttime darkness around the house, and yet Jubal knew Miles had to be peering outwards from down there somewhere.

Leary finally broke the silence by saying, with a lot less breathgone anxiety than before, "Jack; I don't see anythin' over there. Must be your imagination."

"Imagination hell," snarled Miles, evidently stung by that innuendo. "I tell you I saw starlight reflectin' off somethin' over there. Somethin' that sure looked like a carbine barrel."

"Well," pronounced Leary matter-of-factly. "It's not a gun barrel, and that's for damned sure, because if it was, an' if there was anyone over there, they could've shot me by now."

16

WALT AND JUBAL EXCHANGED A WRY LOOK. THEY could indeed have shot Leary by now and the idea was full of merit in their eyes, but they wanted *both* those killers, and to reveal their presence now, even though they got Leary, would also give Jack Miles all the warning he'd need to try for another escape. Neither of them felt like spending the balance of this long and arduous night, plus perhaps another day or two at additional pursuit, so they wordlessly looked back and forth, said nothing, and held their breaths waiting for Miles to get over being spooked.

It was Mike Leary, younger and perhaps therefore more foolhardy, who broke the stalemate. Mike strode up to the edge of the log house, looked around, stepped out into plain sight and said, "Hey, Jack; get rid of your butterflies. There's no one around here. Hell; if there was they'd have cut loose by now."

Miles though, still had his caution. From around the far side of the house he said, "Forget that damned door and come on around here where I am. We need horses, not food. We can shoot a buck or a cow tomorrow. Right now we need those fresh horses, and we need 'em fast. Don't ever kid yourself that by now the good folks of Jefferson aren't buzzin' like a hive full of bees over what happened to Amos Redmond."

Leary gave a big shrug of his rangy shoulders and turned away from the cabin's door. As he walked along he said, "But that door wasn't locked, Jack, an' now it is, which means—"

Miles exasperatedly cursed.

Jubal balanced the notion of trying to go down the front of the house also; of sending Bond around the back to cut those two off. He was forming the necessary words to state his plan when some loping horses made an increasingly loud drumroll of sound from out over the high desert southward. Bond jerked upright enough to see over the brush. "What the hell," he ripped out.

Jubal, who had heard this same sound many times over the past years, said quietly, "My horses coming back to the pool. Come on, Constable, we've got to get back over where we were. They'll make a try now, sure."

The horses whipped on up heightening the dust scent

126

in the air, swerved wide around the buildings and flashed past under the yellow moon heading north-westward. It was their steady thunder which Jubal used to advantage by running as swiftly as he safely could back across the old Indian trail, paying no heed to the amount of noise he made now. Walt Bond also lumbered back across the trail, and Walt, whether he meant not to or just plain couldn't help it, blundered through the undergrowth making nearly as much noise as those playful horses were making.

They got close enough to see the horses race on up into the poolside tall grass and come down to a stiff-legged stop. Several of them playfully crow-hopped, others went down to drink, and that black stud-colt with the sore neck hung back rolling his eyes and making little low snorts with his compressed nostrils. This one, of all the horses, was not going to be slipped up on again at this place. He had his share of aches to remind him of being snared here recently and vividly.

Bond suddenly dropped down and threw out a rigid arm to warn Jubal. Coming stealthily up through the first fringe of trees was a stalking man. It was impossible for the first several hundred feet to discern which of the fugitives this stalker was, but Bond made the identification correctly when he got one good long look at the killer's face where starshine tumbled through a break in the forest.

He put his lips to Jubal's ear. "Leary. He's left his carbine somewhere an' he's got a lariat in his right hand. With a little luck we can nail this one before he can drop that rope and grab his gun."

But luck rarely favors the anxious.

An old mare ambling around the north side of the pool suddenly threw up her head, pointed towards the

127

forest with her ears and snorted. At once every other horse took faint alarm. Leary, seeing this abrupt interest in something in the yonder trees, halted to stand a while as stiff and motionless as a post.

Jubal and Walt Bond had a bad moment. Obviously that old mare had caught their scent. She stood out there staring straight up towards them. Neither of them moved. In fact they scarcely breathed. During this interlude Jack Miles appeared off to the west. Jack had evidently made a deep sweep southward to get far out and around the horses before beginning to stalk them, but Jack had no premonition as yet, he kept moving up, very gently and very silently.

The old mare bobbed her head a few times, Jubal and Constable Bond remained like stone, and eventually, as the other horses, farther back and unable to pick up any man scent, dropped their heads into the pastern-high grass, the old mare also decided there was no immediate danger and turned to amble back the way she'd come.

Bond lifted one hand, brushed Jubal's elbow and said, "They're both in sight now. You take Miles, I'll take Leary. Hold a steady sightin' on them. I'll call out an' if they don't surrender—kill them."

Jubal nodded and carefully raised his carbine.

Jack Miles was almost even with the farthest cottonwoods now. Mike Leary, over eastward in the direction of the buildings, was also close to some trees. Constable Bond waited until Jubal was ready before he raised his own carbine, took a long rest and a good bead, then he hailed those men out there.

"Miles! Leary! Steady now; don't move. You're covered by Winchesters." Bond paused to watch those two shadows suck back instantly and press against tree trunks in sudden astonishment. "Drop your guns and

128

you'll go back to Jefferson astride. Make a fight of this and you'll go back tied face down. Now shed those guns!"

It was now no longer possible to make out either fugitive but Jubal and Bond knew precisely where each killer was and kept their carbines raised and ready.

The stillness went unbroken except for the quick, sharp interest of those milling horses down there at the sound of men's voices in the night around them. But the animals were not unused to this, so except for that spooked black colt they were content to wait and look and listen.

Finally Jack Miles called out. "Is that you, Walt?"

"Yeah it's me, Jack."

"You made good time didn't you?"

"Never mind the talk, Jack, just toss out your gun. And listen to me; you're cut off from your horses and also from those buildings, so if you choose to make a fight of this you're goin' to get the worst of it."

"How's Amos, Walt?"

Bond turned a pained expression towards Jubal and said in a quiet voice, "Thinks he's bein' real cool. Thinks he'll maybe talk his way out of this. Hmph!" Bond faced outward again with his head dropped low over the Winchester he held. "Quit stalling, Jack, and toss out that gun. You too, Leary. You're both covered."

Leary's reply to this came back quickly. "Covered hell, Bond. Unless you got a howitzer up there that can shoot down a tree I'm safer'n you are."

Walt Bond's face turned flinty. At his side Jubal also read the defiance from those two out there by the pool in everything they said. Miles was going to try and make some clever play. Leary, on the other hand, was a different type of man altogether. Leary was fast with a

129

gun; he meant to rely on this deadliness now. Leary wasn't a schemer, he was a fighter.

Jubal lowered his carbine, leaned over and said, "Walt, keep 'em talking. I'll see how far around Miles I can get."

Bond nodded and as Jubal started crawling off, Jack Miles sang out again. "Hey, Walt; why don't you start shootin'? I want to count the guns with you. I've got a feeling it's only you and maybe the last of those Bradens."

"That's enough," responded the lawman sharply. "That's more'n enough to clean you two out."

"Then come and have a try at it," snapped Mike Leary. "Come on, Constable, have a try at it."

Bond was briefly silent. He looked off westerly but Jubal was no longer in sight. He called Leary a name and said, "Jack, that two-bit gunman with you darned well might get you killed. Get smart and quit while you still can."

Leary laughed. It was an ugly sound. To Miles he called out saying, "Jack, I don't believe Braden's with that old fool after all. I think he's plumb alone. Let's work our way up there and part his hair with a bullet."

But Miles, the careful one, neither verbally agreed to this foolhardiness nor offered to move from his shielding tree. He instead called over to Bond in that same smooth tone again. "Walt; you can't nail the three of us. Besides, what's your interest? Amos got knocked over the head but he didn't get killed, so leave it be while you still can ride off."

Bond said, "There aren't three of you, Jack. There are only you and Leary. Cullen's dead. He's inside the house over there." Bond's tone sharpened now as he faced towards Mike Leary. "That door you fellers found

130

locked—we locked it after puttin' Cullen inside to keep varmints from gnawin' on him. And Leary; we could've shot you ten times since the pair of you came back to get fresh horses. Put *that* in your damned pipe and smoke it!"

Leary's tone was slightly altered when he said, "Jack; I was right over at the house; I thought someone had been there after we left."

"That's past history now," snapped Miles. "Hey, Walt; what'll it take to get you to pull out?"

"Your guns, Jack, nothing less."

"You don't leave us much choice," stated Miles.

Bond's answer to this was cold and final. "That's right. No choice at all. Either throw down your guns or get blasted out there."

Leary started to snarl something but over westerly Miles suddenly gave a jump and a loud grunt as Jubal appeared off on Miles's right where the grass was tallest. Miles snapped off a frantic shot at the rising-up apparition he'd caught sight of from the corner of his eye.

Jubal also fired. He was holding his Winchester low and across his sidewards body. Miles gave a little cry and fell back against his protecting tree as he fired twice more driving Jubal flat down in the grass.

Leary opened up on the northward forest. He had a fair notion where Bond was from listening to the talk, but this worked both ways because Bond slammed two hard shots off, and both slugs struck Leary's tree.

These two were absorbed in their individual duel too. Bond had no time to look around and see how Jubal and Jack Miles were making out. If he had perhaps at least part of this sudden battle could have been effectively ended then and there because Miles, seeing that he

131

could not possibly remain where he was, exposed to Jubal's gunfire, began to desperately fling himself from tree to tree in a frantic effort to get around the pool and over where Leary was.

The gunshots stampeded the horses, which, in turn, ruined Jubal's second and third shots at racing Jack Miles. Horses flashed past Jubal where he lay hidden in the tall grass. He flung away from those deadly hooves as he fired, and of course he missed both times.

Miles, Jubal thought, had been struck by that first bullet, and yet the way Jack was fleeing now it didn't appear that the bullet wound was a mortal one.

When the last horse whipped past, Jubal cautiously raised up. A bullet slashed through grass inches to his left. He dropped flat again, cursed, and began crawling southward. Two more bullets probed the grass for him, but each of these deadly harbingers swished through where he had been and not where he now was. Still, Miles had the best of it; at least he had trees to get behind.

Leary and Walt Bond prolonged their fierce duel, but with them it was more nearly a genuine fight to the death. Both remained stationary and both from time to time had to expose a little of themselves in order to get off a shot. Leary had Walt's position pinpointed now; he'd seen every red muzzleblast in the darkness and kept Walt from risking a move with his unerring accuracy. Of the two fugitives, Mike Leary was by far the better gunman.

Jubal rolled southward and kept always near the edge of the pool where grass grew tallest. He pursued Jack Miles steadily, trying to keep pressure on the killer. Miles took a stand once, waited for Jubal to fire, and afterwards he cut through the grass where that crimson

132

Winchester flash had come from with four rapid shots. Jubal though was moving clear even as he fired. Still, one of Miles's bullets plowed along Jubal's upper left arm ripping his shirt and neatly slicing through his skin. Blood gushed. Jubal had to stop long enough to examine that wound. This gave Miles time enough to complete his withdrawal around the pool where Leary was straining to end his part of this fight.

Jubal's injury wasn't serious but the bleeding annoyed him; blood ran down under his sleeve and into his palm making it difficult for him to hold his carbine without constantly wiping one hand upon the ground.

Leary and Miles evidently held a quick discussion of their situation for now they opened up on Constable Bond with their concentrated fire driving the constable flat down over in the forest where he was hidden. He could not even raise up long enough to get off a shot. For nearly a full half-minute those two probed for Bond. Jubal, making a crude tourniquet for his injured arm, watched this furious firing and fervently hoped Bond would not try to raise up to reply to it.

Then Leary and Miles sprang clear of their tree and made a wild run for the yonder buildings. They had their horses over there. They also had much better protection by the log house.

They made it. By the time Walt gingerly raised up to peer around, they were close enough to the buildings to be safe. Jubal, swearing helplessly at the clumsiness of his own fingers at tying off his improvised tourniquet, sat there unable to halt either Leary or Miles.

Bond finally got off one shot, but both men whipped around the log house and were instantly out of sight.

Jubal finished his chore, got up recklessly and started stalking ahead. Bond too arose and advanced, but Bond had plenty of tree cover, at least as far as the Indian trail, so his advance was swiftest. In fact Bond was in place to resume the fight before Jubal was even clear of the pool, and Bond opened up raking the east side of the log house.

Someone around there cried out.

Jubal moved faster making a sharp swishing sound as he passed hastily through the tall grass. He was ahead of the poolside trees when a rifle lanced flame at him from a corner of the house. He dropped flat and rolled. Whoever had fired that shot had obviously got a carbine from his saddle boot, which clearly meant Miles and Leary had their horse and were now preparing to flee.

Bond stepped up his firing again. He was no longer using the Winchester though; each time he fired the duller, deeper roar of a six-gun reverberated into the shattered night.

Jubal got to one knee, made a careful survey of the onward house, saw no moonlight reflections from over there, heaved upright and lumbered ahead almost to the rear of the house. Where he stopped was directly behind the little log smokehouse. Here, he raised his carbine, settled it across a log and waited. A shadow appeared. Jubal squeezed the trigger, the carbine's firing pin fell upon an empty cartridge, and Jubal hurled the empty, useless gun from him in fierce anger,

17

WALT BOND CALLED OUT AGAIN, DURING A LITTLE lull in the fighting. "Jack; I can see both your horses from up here. If you try to reach them I'll cut you down. Now get smart and quit this damned fighting while you're still able."

"Why?" shouted Mike Leary. "So you can haul us back to Jefferson to hang? No dice, old man; you'd better finish the thing here an' now."

Leary punctuated this with a random shot up in the direction of Walt Bond's voice.

Jubal, six-gun in hand, considered trying to get across the intervening distance to the rear of the house. He could see clearly along the north side, but Leary and Miles were either around the front or were along the southernmost side of the building, and with the odds stacked against him, Jubal decided for the time being to remain where he was.

Now, there came a long lull in the fighting. The longer it ran on the more the night's hush and peril deepened. Jubal could see his brother's fresh grave in the ghostly light. He could also see the northward stretch of clearing where for years the Bradens had cut their winter wood.

A long way off, and westward, came the sound of horses running down the night. Up the mountainside towards the peaks a wildcat made its shrill scream. For as long as this stalemate lasted Jubal wondered whether or not Bond had been bluffing about being able to see the fugitives' horses. He eventually got an answer to this: Walt fired a single shot then called out.

"Don't try it again, Leary. The next one'll hit you sure. You made a bad mistake tyin' those horses out in plain sight."

Mike called Walt Bond a fierce name. Evidently Bond's bullet had come uncomfortably close.

The silence settled in again. It drew out tensely and Jubal finally decided to risk reaching the rear of his house. Anything was better than doing nothing at all. He sucked back around the smokehouse, stepped along its

135

little northward wall, drew no fire, saw no movement or reflection, swept in a big breath and started running.

No shots came; evidently Miles and Leary were along the south wall somewhere and were concentrating upon Walt Bond. He flattened against the rough, round logs, held his six-gun low and waited for his breathing to return to normal.

Bond and Leary opened up on one another again. This time, it appeared to Jubal, that Walt had moved again; had darted across the hunter's trail and was now back about where the killers had originally hidden when they had ridden up here to kill his brother. Because he was thoroughly familiar with every inch of the front of the house, the north side of it, and even part of the southward run of land.

A rifle shot ripped out, around the front. Instantly Bond's answering blast crashed in prompt reply. For a moment there was no more shooting. Jubal wondered whether or not the long lulls between shots was directed by the fugitives' dwindling supply of ammunition or not.

Walt Bond, evidently also thinking along these lines, called forth. "Jack? Hey, Jack, you hear me? We can outwait you fellers. Come daylight and there'll be others up here. You can't reach the horses and you can't keep this up indefinitely. Quit while you're still alive."

Miles didn't answer, Mike Leary did, "Constable, I'll make a trade with you. Let me get to my horse and I'll give you Miles."

Jubal began gliding southward along the back wall. He hoped Bond would keep on talking and Bond did. He said, "Is he hit, Leary?"

"Yeah, he's hit. Braden got him over by the pool."

"Then wise up, man. By yourself you don't stand a chance."

"I stand a better chance than ever, Constable. So do you. You want Miles an' I want out of this all in one piece. We make a trade—Miles for my horse. You can take Jack back to Jefferson an' be a big hero. I'll head out of this lousy Oregon country for good. We both get what we want."

"No dice, Mike," replied Bond. "How bad's Jack hurt?"

"Bad enough unless he gets patched up pretty soon."

"Then throw down your gun, Leary. By yourself you can't possibly get clear."

"Yeah?" called the killer. "You forgettin' Braden's no longer fightin' alongside you, Bond? He hasn't fired a shot since those damned horses run over the top of him. It's just you'n me now, Constable, so let's make our trade. No one else'll ever know."

Walt Bond stopped talking. Jubal thought he understood Walt's problem; the constable was suddenly trying to recall when Jubal had last been seen or heard from. Up to now Bond had been wholly absorbed in his own end of the fight. Now, after what Leary had said, he was undoubtedly wondering whether what Leary had implied was true or not.

But what occurred to Jubal was not whether Bond believed he was out of the fight; what intrigued him as he halted near the edge of the house, was whether *Leary* believed this or not, because if Leary *did* believe it, then he wouldn't be expecting a sudden attack from behind.

Walt said: "Leary, you're mistaken. Jubal's stalkin' you right this minute from over by the pool."

Leary made that harsh, ugly little laugh of his. Now it rang with scornful derision. "Try again, Constable."

"Leary? Tell Jack to come on out where I can see him. If he's bad hurt I can maybe help him."

For a moment Leary was silent. Jubal, near the dangerous corner of the house heard two low voices around there. One unmistakably belonging to Leary. The other, less recognizable because it was too low and too slurred, had to belong to Miles. Jubal took the final step which placed him within inches of being able to peer around the corner of his house. He gathered himself for the leap, but suddenly held off because Leary was speaking again.

"Bond? All right; I send you Jack an' you pass me your word you'll hold off while I go for my horse."

Walt swore at Leary. "I told you before—no dice."

"Then Jack bleeds to death around here, Bond."

"Tie off the bleedin', Leary."

"I can't. It's in his side. Hey, Bond; you deliberately goin' to let him die like this?"

If Mike Leary thought he had Walt Bond over a barrel the constable's reply to his last question dispelled this illusion. "He can die any old way he wants to, Leary. He's no good, never was any good, and if he dies up here it'll only save Jefferson the cost of a trial an' a hangin'."

Leary fired two rapid, wrathful shots at the sound of Bond's voice. That was when Jubal decided Leary would be too otherwise occupied to be watching behind himself, and took two big thrusting steps around the corner of the house, his cocked six-gun swinging in search of a target.

There was no target. Neither Leary nor Jack Miles were alongside the house and in one swift glance Jubal saw why this was so. A window in the south wall was open; there were scuff marks where two sets of boots had hurriedly scrambled up over the round logs. He dropped down at once and lunged inward to get flat

138

alongside that same wall. He made it safely because Bond and Leary began their renewed duel again.

For as long as that firing continued Jubal lay there thinking. There was one possible way to end this. He crawled over to the window, got both legs up under him and waited for Leary to fire again. When he did, Jubal shot straight upwards in front of the window, poked his six-gun through and frantically sought the man-shape which had to be close by, firing through a front window. It was very dark inside the house. Something rustled off on Jubal's left. He swung. A six-gun was slowly lifting towards him. He had no time to determine whether this was Leary or Jack Miles; he had only time enough to whip his gun hand around and squeeze the trigger, lifted the hammer and squeeze again. Those two hand gun shots lit up the inside with a dazzling crimson brilliance and a noise as deafening as cannon fire. There was also a third shot, from inside, but that muzzle blast went straight upwards into the ceiling, for the hand holding this other gun was already jerking wildly from the impact of two bullets.

Someone inside the house let off a sudden, sharp howl. Jubal was dropping when that man cried out. He was below the windowsill when a belated gunshot thundered from over near the inside front wall where Mike Leary had evidently been caught entirely by surprise.

It took a moment for the echoes to die away. It also took a moment for Leary's smarting eyes to recover from that searing brilliance inside the otherwise pitch-dark house. Jubal used that brief respite to duck back around the corner to the rear of the house again.

Suddenly Walt Bond's exultant voice cried over to Leary. "Hey, Mike; what's got into you over there? Did

139

Braden get you that time?" Bond laughed. "Still think he's out of it?"

Leary's answer was unprintable.

Bond waited a moment then said, "You stop a little lead too, Leary; you had enough now?"

"Not by a damned sight," yelled the outlaw. "And Braden's a lousy shot. He missed me completely an' finished off Miles. So nothing's changed, Bond, damn your lousy soul, except that now I know where Braden is too."

Jubal kept silent. He methodically shucked out his spent six-gun casings and plugged in fresh loads from his depleted shell belt. So he had killed Jack Miles; it didn't exhilarate him particularly, finding this out, but it gave him a bleak sense of satisfaction. His brother had now been avenged.

He closed the loading gate of his .45, cocked the weapon and settled a moment to deeply breathe the cool night air. Two dead and one still living. Cullen and Miles accounted for. The deadliest of the trio still defiant and fighting. He wanted Mike Leary as badly as he'd wanted Jack Miles. For Will Cullen he'd never felt anything but a cold, steady contempt.

Constable Bond fired a shot around the front and Jubal heard window glass tinkle. He also heard Leary throw back an answering gunshot, and for only a moment longer he lingered back there, relaxed and easy, then he began to move, not southward back where that open window was, but northward up around the house where he could see the place that Walt Bond was using as his vantage point.

When he got around there he called out to Bond, his voice low and his words distinct. "Constable; I'm going to burn him out. We'll need the flames to see him by

140

when he runs out. You stay over there and keep watch' round front. I'll keep watch around back."

Bond didn't reply right away but Leary did. He said, "Braden; it's your house—burn it if you like. But there's a heap of stuff in here it took a lot of sweat to haul up here. As for pickin' me off by firelight—don't bet on it. I've been in tougher spots than this in my life."

"There's an end to every road, Leary," called Jubal. "You've come to yours here and now."

"Like hell," snarled Leary. "If things get too hot I'll just toss out my gun."

Jubal said quietly, "That isn't going to save you, Leary. I'll kill you armed or unarmed. If you don't believe that try surrendering and walking out of there."

For a space of several seconds Leary was silent. Then he called over to Constable Bond. "Hey, lawman; you hear what Braden just said? You goin' to be a party to a murder?"

Bond's reply was laconic. "Leary; a while back you said only you an' I'd know how this thing ended. Well; it looks like you were a little wrong: Only *Braden* and I will know."

Leary said no more and Jubal, correctly assuming he had inspired the fugitive towards some desperate fresh effort, moved back around behind the house to be in position to see Leary should the gunman try escaping back out of the house by that southward window.

The night was well advanced now, the starshine was softly brilliant and the old yellow moon was halfway down its westerly descent. A steady cool breeze was blowing from the heights bearing with it a strong, acrid scent of cooling rock and curing forage grasses. Somewhere far down the distant northward slopes a beautiful girl and an anxious town were awaiting the outcome of this chase, this

141

fight to the death. Jubal had an idea those men down in Jefferson would be unable to resist the urge to form into a posse and come over the mountains to investigate, but he doubted very much that they would arrive before dawn or perhaps even later, and by then, he was convinced, all the fighting would be ended.

18

FOR A LONG WHILE, PERHAPS FIFTEEN MINUTES, THERE was no more shooting. Leary, still in the log house with his dead companions, had to be doing some serious thinking. It would require no vast intelligence for a man in his situation to realize the utter futility of continued resistance. Neither would it require any great amount of perception for him to understand that unless he could surrender to the constable from Jefferson City he was going to get killed by Jubal Braden.

As for Walt Bond in his yonder thicket, he was as quiet as a mouse over there. Jubal thought Walt would be using this long rest to reload and be ready when the fight was renewed.

As for himself, Jubal had no longer any doubts about the ending of this battle. His guns were freshly loaded and he was ready; was waiting with the powerful patience which was so much a part of his fatalistic philosophy for Leary to make his next move.

But the time ran on, Leary was quiet in there, and a little cool chill came into the night. It was late now, much later than Jubal thought. The moon was far down the western sky, the world was utterly hushed.

Leary called over to Walter Bond. "Constable? Listen to me: I'll surrender. You hear?"

"I hear," said Bond.

"All right, you listen. I'll surrender to *you*—not to Braden, an' don't you have him nowhere around when I come out. I want your word on that."

Bond was briefly silent. He appeared to be considering Leary's offer and its alternatives. Finally he said, "Leary; the only thing I'll promise you is that if you throw out your gun right now and step through the front door of that house, I'll do everything I can to protect you."

Leary said no more for a while. Around the back, Jubal hefted his six-gun, turned and stepped over to the north corner of the house to peer up there where Bond was crouching out of sight.

Walt called down to him. "Jubal; you heard. What'd you say; you goin' to leave it in my hands or not?"

Jubal kept watching that eastward underbrush while he thought on this. What eventually swayed him in favor of letting Bond have his way was two factors. One; he'd had enough killing. He'd looked upon two dying men this night and despite his cold vengefulness the fierce motivation which had influenced him up to this final moment, was somewhat blunted. The second factor complemented the first one. Whether he killed Leary or not, the youthful gunman was going to die. They'd hang him sure, down in Jefferson; frontier justice in a lawless land was apt to be as abrupt and unrelenting in a fair trial as it also was when left to the individual.

"All right," he called over to Bond. "You can have him."

Leary had evidently been awaiting that answer as much as Walt Bond also had, because Leary said at once: "No tricks now, Braden, damn you. Hey,

Constable; you heard him. But all the same you watch him close. I don't trust him one cussed bit."

"You can trust him," rejoined Bond briskly. "Toss out your gun and come out of there with both hands high, Leary."

Jubal heard movement inside. He glided up to the front corner of the northward wall and flattened there listening for the door latch to be lifted. When it eventually made its oaken sound and the door creaked inwards, Jubal settled flat down in his boots.

"Bond?" called Leary. "Where's Braden? I ain't comin' out of here until he's in plain sight where you can cover him."

Walt swore exasperatedly. "For a tough guy, Leary, you're sure all of a sudden gettin' careful. Just walk out of there. I can see Braden an' I got him covered. But his word's good with me. Now come on out of there."

Leary walked out with both hands above his head. He paused just beyond the doorway swinging his head left and right obviously looking for Jubal. When he did not at once see him, Leary took several further steps into the star brightened dusty yard.

Jubal moved around the corner of the house and was behind Leary as well as northward of him. He had his six-gun trained upon the killer. Leary finally saw him up there and stopped dead still.

"Bond; you watch him now," called Leary, his eyes boring into Jubal.

Walt stood up out of the thicket which had shielded him. He too had a levelled six-gun in his hand. He brushed through into the clearing and started ahead towards the fugitive. Jubal hadn't moved; he was watching Leary with his full attention. When Bond got up to the outlaw he squinted at Leary's empty holster,

144

squinted up into the killer's boyish face, let off a big breath and eased down the hammer of his weapon, lowered his right hand and dropped the gun into its hip holster.

That was when Leary made his move. He had Bond two feet in front of him empty handed. Off on his right was his patient standing horse. On his left off a goodly distance stood Jubal. With one swift forward lunge Leary grabbed Walt Bond and whirled him towards Jubal, who dared not fire. Leary hung to Bond with all the strength of one arm while he plunged a hand towards Walt's holstered .45. It had all been obviously carefully thought out before Leary had even walked out of the house. He'd realized his chances were nil as long as he continued fighting inside the house. He also knew that if he could catch either one of his enemies as a hostage, the other one wouldn't dare fire on him.

It was a smooth maneuver and except for one thing probably would have succeeded. What Leary had overlooked was the physical fact that lanky and rangy and quick as he was, he was no match in physical strength for either Jubal Braden or doughty, short, compact, very powerful Walt Bond.

In fact, even before Jubal lurched ahead, Leary had to abandon his groping for Bond's six-gun because the muscular constable was whip-sawing with all his considerable strength forcing Leary to hang onto him with both hands or get flung clear.

With a wild curse Leary clubbed Bond over the head with one balled fist. He kneed the lawman in the back and he got half a stranglehold around Bond's throat. All of these things hurt Bond but none of them stunned him; he bowed his back and dropped far over

145

lifting Leary off the ground. He reached backwards, caught clothing, and tried to spin Leary around.

Leary finally staked his last chance on one wild attempt to get Bond's six-gun. He let go and dropped down, going for that right hand holster. Bond, evidently feeling the gun being wrenched clear, threw himself downwards and sidewards at the same time he cried a warning to Jubal who was rushing the killer.

Jubal fired. A red lash of flame nearly blinded Walt Bond as he struck the ground and frantically rolled. There was another burst of gun thunder and crimson flame, this time from Leary. Jubal was less than twenty feet away when he got off his second shot. Leary gasped. Jubal lifted his hammer, kept the trigger depressed and let his thumb slide off the hammer for his third shot. That time Mike Leary fell. But he hung there on all fours trying to lift his gun. Jubal fired his fourth and final shot. Leary crumpled, slid forward his full length and lay completely loose in the ghostly night.

Jubal covered the little intervening distance with his thrusting stride, toed Leary over onto his back and gazed at him as he methodically began punching out spent casings and feeling along his shell-belt for the last bullets in his depleted loops.

Bond struggled back to his feet, beat dust off himself with his crumpled hat, shot a look up at Jubal, shot a longer look downwards at dead Mike Leary, and moved ahead to retrieve his six-gun from near Leary's body.

"Sorry," he muttered, greatly chagrined. "If he'd killed you it'd have been more my fault than his."

Jubal drew in an unsteady breath. "It wasn't your fault, Walt. A man expects another man to keep his word. Even a rotten whelp like this one."

"No; that's no excuse, Jubal. There isn't any excuse. It was my fault from start to finish."

"Well," murmured Jubal putting up his gun and turning his back on Mike Leary, "it's over now an' I reckon that's what counts, Walt."

"Yeah, I reckon. Jubal?"

"Yes."

"It happened the best way for all of us. Any other way there would've been second thoughts down the years. You know what I mean?"

"Yeah, I know. But if I never have to do anything like this again it'll suit me right down to the ground."

They went over to the front of the cabin and dropped down over there in the dusty moonlight, two very tired, exhausted and drained dry men, one young, one not so young, but for this little time both of them feeling ancient and weary beyond redemption.

After Bond reloaded his gun and craned around for a look inside through the open door, he said, "You know; I don't think Leary or Miles ever even saw Cullen in there with them."

"It was too dark," stated Jubal. "They didn't have the time to go poking around."

Bond fished for his tobacco sack, went to work twisting up a cigarette and afterwards offered the makings to Jubal, who shook his head and continued to sit there with both long arms limply balanced over his knees, large-knuckled hands hanging limply downwards. Walt lit up, exhaled, deeply inhaled and lifted his head enough to blow a bluish streamer straight up at the paling sky.

"Reckon we ought to start back," he muttered, his thoughts slowly coming back to the present and its detailed demands. "Jack's horse and Leary's horse are

147

tied yonder, still, but I suppose by now Cullen's animal's gone out on the high desert to join your horses."

"I'll catch him in a little while," stated Jubal. "Right now I'd just like to sit here for a spell."

"Sure."

They sat for almost an hour and by then there was a paleness to the eastern rims. When they finally shrugged back up to their feet though, Jubal suddenly grunted and whipped around northward.

"Horsemen coming," he said, all that former lethargy gone in a flash.

Bond listened and nodded and said, "Folks from town more'n likely."

It was; thirteen men from Jefferson armed to the teeth, and one girl also armed: Mary Bond.

They came slowly down into the yard with false dawn all around them. They halted within sight of Walt and Jubal, and dead Mike Leary. They murmured small greetings and got stiffly down. They'd been in the saddle since late the night before.

At sight of his daughter Constable Bond walked over to her, that stub of a cigarette dead between his lips. It bobbed when he spoke.

"Honey; what're you doin' up here?"

Mary looked long at her father's sweat-streaked, dirty and whiskery features. She softly smiled. "Just came along to be sure you were warmly dressed. It's cold at dawn, isn't it?"

Walt said no more.

Over where Leary lay men stood strongly silent and assessing. One of them murmured something to Jubal. He pointed towards the cabin's open door and said nothing aloud. The men trooped on over and went inside. They emerged moments later and looked inquiringly at Constable Bond.

Walt nodded at them. "We'll need three horses to take 'em back on. Two are yonder—those ones already saddled. The other one's wanderin' around . . ."

"Sure," exclaimed a bearded townsman softly. "We'll fetch him, Walt. You'n Mister Braden just set a spell." As this man turned to give brief orders to his companions Walt walked over closer to him.

"How's Amos?" he asked.

The bearded man faced back around and gently nodded. "He'll do, Walt. He'll do. But it'll be a few weeks before he'll be able to find a hat that'll fit him."

Mary Bond strolled across where Jubal was quietly standing near the fresh turned earth of young John's grave. He turned at the sound of her and looked down. She made an uncertain little smile up at him,

"You said you'd take care of my father and you did. I want to thank you."

Jubal shrugged. "I'm not sure, ma'am, about just who looked out for whom."

She dropped her gaze to the grave then lifted it again. "Will you be coming back with us, Mister Braden?"

Jubal hadn't thought ahead this far yet and now, as he did, he was silent. Mary Bond, studying his rugged profile, thought she could understand how this big man felt. She put forth a hand to touch his hand, to hold his fingers in a tight, brief grip. She said, "Please ride back with us. Stay in town for a week or so."

He lowered his tired gaze. "Why, ma'am?"

"Right now it won't be any good—staying up here by yourself. Then too, there's your father's funeral."

Jubal nodded. "I'd forgotten that. I reckon I'm more tired than I figured I was."

"It's been a long night for the rest of us as well. Mister Braden . . . ?"

"Yes'm."

"This is a beautiful spot up here. I had no idea the high desert country could be like this."

"Have you ever been up here before, Miss Mary?"

"No. Father always said some day we'd pack a horse and come up here for a few days."

Jubal turned so that his back was to his brother's grave. He nodded off easterly in the direction of Blueberry Camp. The fading moon and its raffish little stars were shading that eastern world a steely blue now, and somewhere just beyond the horizon a faint golden brightness was firming up.

"It's a big country, ma'am."

"And a—lonely one, Mister Braden?"

He looked at her. "Yes'm. And also a lonely one."

"If my father and I came up here sometime, could you take a day or two off to show it to us?"

Jubal glanced over where Walt and the others were busily engaged with three horses and three canvas-wrapped long bundles. He stepped around to block out this grisly scene and nodded. "I'll be lookin' forward to that day, Miss Mary. You reckon it'll be soon?"

She smiled into his eyes. "Very soon, Mister Braden. Just as soon as—other things—have become memory. Perhaps two or three weeks. Would that be all right?"

"That would be fine," he said. "I'll fetch your paw's horse and mine; they're up in the trees. Maybe you and I could start out a little ahead of the others."

"Yes," murmured lovely Mary Bond, and as Jubal turned to stride away she went over to her father, spoke quietly to him, then walked back out a way to await Jubal's return.

Walt Bond, supervising the lashing of three dead men across their saddles, turned and for a long time gazed out where his daughter was watching Jubal return with the horses. For the first time in several days Walt's face was gently thoughtful and composed.

We hope that you enjoyed reading this
Sagebrush Large Print Western.
If you would like to read more Sagebrush titles,
ask your librarian or contact the Publishers:

United States and Canada

Thomas T. Beeler, *Publisher*
Post Office Box 659
Hampton Falls, New Hampshire 03844-0659
(800) 818-7574

United Kingdom, Eire, and
the Republic of South Africa

Isis Publishing Ltd
7 Centermead
Osney Mead
Oxford OX2 0ES England
(01865) 250333

Australia and New Zealand

Bolinda Publishing Pty. Ltd.
17 Mohr Street
Tullamarine, 3043, Victoria, Australia
(016103) 9338 0666